Chapati and Chips

Almas Khan

Springboard

1993

Published by Yorkshire Art Circus
School Lane, Glass Houghton, Castleford
West Yorkshire, WF10 4QH
Telephone (0977) 550401

Typeset by Yorkshire Art Circus
Printed by FM Reprographics, Roberttown

ISBN 0 947780 99 8
Classification: Fiction

Springboard is the fiction imprint of Yorkshire Art Circus. We work to increase access to writing and publishing and to develop new models of practice for arts in the community.
For details of the full programme of Yorkshire Art Circus workshops and our current book list, please write to the address above.

Yorkshire Art Circus is a registered charity (number 1007443)

Acknowledgements:
Olive Fowler
Reini Schühle

This book is dedicated to Almas's mother and father.

We would like to thank the following organisations for support towards this book:

PART ONE

Trouble In t'Family

Sure I was only a kid, but when you're small you remember things that adults tend to forget.

It was raining outside, so Arif, my cousin, and I had decided to adjust my bike in the hallway.

'Keep the noise down,' Mum said from the kitchen.

The bell rang, two sharp rings. Arif ran to the door and unlocked it. 'Wow, a cop!' he said loudly.

'Hello, can I come in?'

Mum came out of the kitchen. 'Who is it, Arif?'

'Aunt Carla, there's a cop out here.'

Mum rushed towards the door, wiping her hands on her apron. 'Can I help you?'

'Is it alright if I step inside?'

'Please do, 'Mum gestured with her hands. 'What can I do for you?'

'Are you Mrs Malik?' The cop took off his wet helmet.

Mum nodded silently and led him into the living room. Arif closed the front door and then helped me to lean my bike against the wall. He'd been green with envy when Mum and Dad had bought it for me on my ninth birthday.

'Give us a go, Stacey.'

'Why should I? This is my bike. Look how shiny the red paint is and the seat's so soft.'

'Be a sport. Let me have one turn.'

But I never would.

The accidents I had on that bike. Everytime I crashed into a wall or fell off and grazed my knees, Dad would laugh and say, 'Come on, love. I thought you were made of tougher stuff. Have another go.'

I watched Arif run his hands slowly across the seat, I knew what he was thinking. 'Come on,' I said . 'Let's find out what the cop wants.'

We went into the living room, Mum held out her hand to me. I went over and sat down. Arif stood by the door, his eyes fixed on the cop.

The cop cleared his throat. 'Mrs Malik, I don't know how to say this. There was an accident.'

Mum's hand shot to her mouth. 'What kind of an accident?'

'Your husband was involved in a road accident.'

Mum moaned softly.

'I'm sorry, Mrs Malik, your husband died.'

As long as I live, I'll never forget the look of raw pain on Mum's face. Or the way my own heart seemed to stop beating.

Surely there had to be a mistake. The cop must have got it wrong. He sat there, helmet in hand, and kept saying 'Sorry,' over and over again. That wasn't going to bring my dad back.

Everything happened in slow motion. I couldn't speak. My tongue had turned to wood in my mouth. Arif sank to the floor and sat with his hands covering his face. He was crying softly.

Mum, deathly pale, got to her feet slowly.

'We'll need you to come to the hospital to identify the body.'

Mum nodded. 'Give me some time to sort out the children.'

After he left, Mum burst into tears. She cried until she was exhausted and then said she was going to get Arif's Dad, Uncle Naveed, to drop her off at the hospital.

'Mum, take me with you,' I pleaded.

She shook her head. 'Darling, I can't. Stay here with Arif and be a good girl for me.' Her face was as white as a sheet. She 'phoned Uncle Naveed. I can't understand why she was so calm. She knew what she had to do.

Aunt Razia and Uncle Naveed came over to our house straightaway. Aunt Razia hugged Mum and led her out to the car.

Nothing mattered anymore. I bumped into my bike as I went to watch them drive away. It fell with a loud crash. The back wheel span round and round.

I moved slowly from room to room, like an automaton. Arif followed me, he tried to speak but, surprisingly, words had failed him also.

Dad wasn't coming home. He'd left us forever! How could my dad be dead? Why, only that morning, he'd tousled my hair and promised to take me to the chip shop after work.

I can still remember that I couldn't cry. I felt totally cut off from the rest of the world. In my own mind there was nothing but silence. Like a zombie I watched those around me lose control and breakdown. Anger made me maintain the stiff upper lip that Granddad insisted was the hallmark of the British. Only the weak and helpless cried. And tragically, I was both.

Mum needed a crutch. Somebody to lean on, and in her own anguish she seemed to forget I existed. People came and went, expressing their sorrow and walking away.

Mum had lost her husband. But what about me? Dad had been my hero, my friend and confidant. Life could never be the same without him. Uncle Naveed and Arif accompanied Dad's coffin to Pakistan. As the men lifted it into the car, I tried to stop them. I still couldn't cry and felt as though a huge lock had been fitted around my heart and the key had been misplaced.

Just when I thought that things couldn't get any worse Mum went and dropped a bombshell. Granddad was moving in. How did she expect me to live with him when he hated my guts?

For it all to make sense, I'll have to go back to when all the trouble in t'family began.

My dad was a muslim from Pakistan and Mum's white. She was born in 1945, the only child of Arthur and Ethel Harris. Being an only child was a disadvantage. Mum didn't have many friends of her own, so that meant a very lonely existence over the top of a grocery store in Bradford.

My grandparents were quite strict with her. She had to go straight to school and return home without dilly-dallying along the way. Weekends and holidays were spent working in the shop for pocket money.

Grandma Ethel died in 1955 after a long illness brought on by a chest infection. Poor Mum! She was left alone at a time when she needed a mother's presence. Granddad Arthur was a right tyrant. He ruled Mum with an iron rod and always tried to live her life for her. Mum had become so used to him running the show she never had the guts to refuse him anything. He got a perverse pleasure from making her miserable.

Mum left school when she was sixteen and Granddad, as usual, had her whole future clearly mapped out for her. He insisted she go to college and do a teacher training course. I have to say that Mum was not very ambitious. She wanted to stay at home and take care of Granddad but he always got his own way and she had no choice but to oblige.

Mum hated college. She said she didn't fit in. She saw there was only one way of getting what she wanted - beating Granddad at his own game. On the pretext of attending college, she got herself a job in Woolworths. Mum was pleased she'd managed to find her independence without upsetting him. Unfortunately, while shopping for groceries, one of the neighbours couldn't resist letting it drop that Carla Harris had a job in Woolworths. Granddad blew his top. He was in a rage when Mum got home from work. They had their first major disagreement and didn't speak for ages.

Granddad was full of resentment and didn't like the way Mum had deceived him. Mum decided it was high time to break new ground and make a life of her own. But deep down in her heart she knew Granddad would never let her go. He had an awful habit of turning a situation around and making himself out to be the victim! Mum was gullible. She always fell for his sob story.

Just to please him and settle their argument, she offered her services in the shop full-time. The tight-fisted old toad jumped at such a golden opportunity and took her up on her offer. At least he didn't have to pay an outsider to do the work that flesh and blood could do for free.

In 1965, Mum met a man! Big deal, you may say. For Mum, it was the best thing that ever happened. The man of her dreams was called Waheed Malik. He was from Pakistan and worked in a textile mill. On the way home from work, he used to stop at the shop for groceries. One thing led to another and before long Mum was absolutely dippy about him.

She couldn't tell Granddad about her boyfriend because all hell would break loose when he discovered that his pride and joy was going out with a 'coloured' man. She kept her secret under wraps until the strain of sneaking about began to get to her.

One evening over supper Mum told Granddad she had a boyfriend. Of course he wanted all the details. Where did he work? What was he like? Were his intentions honourable? And the biggest and most important thing was, did he have bags of money?

Mum replied in the best possible way. Her boyfriend had a good job and wanted to marry her. His name was Waheed.

'Waheed? What kind of a name is that?' he asked.

'He's a Pakistani.'

Granddad almost choked on his pork chop. 'A bloody Paki, you've got to be joking! No daughter of mine is going to marry a Paki.'

Granddad was the biggest racist that ever lived in Bradford. The sort of man who went around saying 'An Englishman's home is his castle.'I bet he'd never seen the interior of one in his whole bloody life!

Mum didn't want to argue with him. 'I want your blessing, Dad.'

'You'll not get that lass! Over my dead body. I'll never forgive you if you marry a Paki.'

That cheeky trash bag. He had the nerve to call my dad a Paki! I tell you there's nobody as ignorant as a white guy who happens to be your granddad and thinks his opinion is the only one that counts. Granddad was a meddling old fool.

No matter how much Mum tried to persuade him to change his way of thinking, that idiot refused to budge. If Mum wanted to throw away her life on a Paki, she had to leave his house in order to do so. Mum was torn two ways. She loved her dad. He'd taken care of her when her mum had died and he'd been good to her. She also loved Waheed. He was everything she desired in a man. And he could give her some security which was what Mum wanted more than anything else.

Granddad tried to talk Mum out of seeing Waheed and he had all sorts of reasons to put her off. Pakis were ignorant, they had no common sense at all and they were useless. They were only allowed into the country because somebody had to keep the mills running. Dirty work for dirty Pakis!

Mum gave the matter considerable thought and then she accepted Waheed's marriage proposal.

Granddad went wild. 'Pack your stuff and sling your hook, you ungrateful baggage. Don't you dare set foot in my house again.'

Mum did the one thing he thought she'd never have the guts to do. She left home.

On January tenth, 1966, she married Waheed. Granddad wasn't there to give her away. My Uncle Naveed stepped in and did the honours.

In July 1967 I made my entry into the world. For my parents I brought joy. Granddad, however, was disgusted. His daughter had given birth to an alien breed! I was a thorn in his side, the constant reminder of his daughter's foolish behaviour, and he despised me.

Mum wanted to call me Stacey. Dad liked Shaheen. They were undecided so Uncle Naveed suggested they call me Stacey Shaheen Malik. And they did.

Granddad also had quite an endearing name for me which he used on several occasions. The cheeky old git called me 'Paki Burger'.

I grew up in a weird atmosphere; there was always something wrong and I became the main topic of conversation. Dad wanted to bring me up without the question mark of religion and cultural background hanging over my head. He told Mum it was up to me to decide what I wanted to do when I was old enough to know right from wrong.

That didn't go down too well with Uncle Naveed and Aunt Razia because they were teaching Arif Islam. Dad refused to discuss it with them. I can't understand why he was so slack when it came to paving out my future.

Granddad, unable to stomach the thought of Mum making a go of things without including him in her plans, began to worm his way into her affections. He had a warped sense of reality. One morning Mum took me out for a walk and we bumped into Granddad on the way. He told Mum she was free to move back in with him if she wanted. But she had to finish with Dad and get rid of me. Then, rather cruelly, he pinched my cheek. I burst into tears and screamed my head off all the way home.

In 1969, we moved into a terraced house on Oak Lane. I have very fond memories of my dad, he was a tall man who had a thick mop of dark black, curly hair. His eyes were hazel and he had the nicest laugh I ever heard. After a hard day working his guts out in the mill, he would come home tired and hungry and still find the energy to entertain me with tales of life in Pakistan. He promised to take me when I was older. We would go for walks in the park and I'd play with the other children while Dad kept a watchful eye on me.

Fridays were my favourite day because Dad would get off work early and we'd go out and buy fish and chips for tea. Dad liked eating them with chapatis. Mum used to call him a 'chapati-chomping monster'.

The fact that I was a girl didn't seem to bother Dad. He was proud of me. Uncle Naveed's son, Arif, who is a year older than me used to play football with us. He didn't think it was a game for girls and would always try to get rid of me. 'Get lost, Stacey, you're a girl, aren't you?'

Thankfully, I had very little contact with Granddad while I was very young. On the few occasions we happened to meet, his tongue was sharpened like a bloody knife. He couldn't resist having a go at Mum. She, being the soft-natured type, would burst into tears. I hated him and formed the conclusion that a visit to Granddad meant only one thing. Trouble!

How Mum ever hit on the idea of letting Granddad move in, I'll never know. I wanted to throttle him. Dad was dead and he got the one thing that he'd always wanted. His daughter back!

I needed attention and, with him around, there was no way I was going to get it. I had nightmares after Dad's death and slept with Mum in her room. I got into trouble at school, she was there to bail me out. I tried everything I could think of to keep Mum to myself. It didn't help. Granddad still moved in.

He was always picking on me and trying to fill Mum's head with nonsense. He wanted her to find herself another man. Enough time had been wasted slaving for a Paki and taking care of his offspring. Granddad was a pain in the rear. I often wished it had been him who'd been killed instead of Dad.

Before I could get on with my life, I had to get rid of the raw ache inside me left behind by Dad. One afternoon, purely by accident, I stumbled on a way to do that. I sat staring at a photograph of Dad for what seemed like an age. I was certain that his features changed. A huge lump stuck in my throat. Tears pricked my eyes and began a steady descent down my cheeks. Hugging the photograph close I cried until all the anguish of the past few months faded.

All the same, by the time I got to upper school I was an emotional mess! I hated school as much as I hated Granddad. Homework was like a death sentence hanging over my head and every evening I died. I'm a bit of a troublemaker so don't be surprised when I tell you I had many a painful punch-up. I'm positive I spent half of my school life being hauled into the head's office.

9

The other girls teased me. They were a mixed bunch. Not one of them had a white Mum. Names like 'Dolly Mixture' and 'Black and White Minstrel' were all the rage.

Luckily for me, I inherited Dad's hair and eye-colouring along with Mum's stubby nose and fair complexion. I was popular with the boys even if the girls hated me. Every time I walked along the corridor, I'd get called a 'slag'.

Taunts of that nature were a red rag dangled in front of a mad bull. I was not a saint. My fuse has always been short and foolish pride saw to it I never walked away from a fight. When I think about it now, I must have been like a bloody idiot sitting on thorns and pretending I couldn't feel the anguish they caused my behind!

My reports were the worst on earth. I'm talking bad! The number of times I changed my report card makes me blush. Getting a grade D was fine by me. It was so much easier to turn it into a B.

Mum would say, 'Well done, Stacey. I'm so proud of you.' Her beautiful smile beaming at me would make me guilty. For a day or two, I'd go around feeling like the scum of the planet for deceiving her. God alone knows how I managed to pass my exams. Revision was as welcome as catching a 'flu bug. I preferred to watch television.

Just in case you're interested, I got five CSEs.

Mum wasn't impressed. 'Stacey, I expected you to do better than this,' she jabbed my certificate with her index finger. 'You always came home with such good results.'

Granddad had to stir. 'She's been lazing around all day. Is it any wonder she got such disgusting results? Kids these days don't know what hard work is.'

I scowled at him and bit my tongue. It was certainly none of his business. He had no right sticking his nose into my affairs.

It seemed I had nothing to work for, there was nobody to impress. Mum cooled down after a while so I had no worries, and to tell you the truth I didn't give a damn about Granddad. He could rot in hell for all I cared!

But I was over the moon when I left school for good. It was time for fun and games now there was no more homework and early nights. My happiness was short-lived. The bubble of bliss burst a few days later. I was bored out of my brains. School had given me a reason to drag myself out of bed in the mornings. Jobs were as rare as hens' teeth. I slouched about the house feeling sorry for myself.

With Mum out of the way from eight in the morning until six in the evening - she worked in a bakery - I was forced to put up with Granddad and his overbearing presence. He couldn't stand me sitting in front of the telly all day and moaned to Mum when she came home.

'You should tell her to get a job, she's a lazy, good-for- nothing girl. Make sure that she pulls her weight.'

He was a fine one to talk! I'd just left school and intended to relax without that old fool breathing down my neck all the time.

The prospect of being jobless and on the dole wasn't exactly riveting. Did I have a choice? No way! Like millions of other poor sods, I ended up signing on.

Granddad, the tight-fisted old git, insisted I pay board. We were eating supper when he said, 'Carla, I think it's time Stacey put some money in the kitty.'

Mum held her fork in mid-air. 'She doesn't get all that much. I'm sure we can manage.'

'Rubbish!' he scoffed through a mouthful of mashed potato. 'Don't let her get off so easily. She's got money and I say she should help out.'

Mum looked uncomfortable. My temper began to rise.

Granddad glared at me. 'You shouldn't be so selfish!' he informed me. 'It's only fair that you donate some money towards food and board.'

'Okay. I will as soon as you hand over your pension.'

Granddad spluttered, 'Don't you give me none of your cheek. You'll end up with a thick ear if you're not careful!'

I shoved back my chair.

'Where are you going?' Mum asked. 'You haven't had your pudding yet.'

'Give it to him! He's the one who doesn't want me to eat. I'm off out.'

Mum was such a caring person. It seemed like she'd always be the same no matter what happened. Dad had given her a reason to enjoy her life and now that he was no longer around, she didn't care who ran the show for her.

Granddad was forever telling her what to do. 'That Waheed's not around anymore, Carla. You should make something for yourself now. Don't cling to the past.'

He was such a pain! I couldn't bear to listen to his jibes about Dad.

Mum would answer, 'Dad, don't rush me. I'll never be able to find a man to take Waheed's place.'

'Rubbish, rubbish girl! It's time you stopped stagnating.'

Mum didn't object to Granddad's treatment, but I did! There was no way I was going to stay under the same roof as him. He stretched my patience to the limit.

There was a course at Bradford College that appealed to me. After discussing it with my cousin, Sameena, I took the plunge. Learning to type and use computers sounded like good fun.

While I was at college, I met Hasan. What a snake he turned out to be! He had looks and charm and he knew how to use them both. God alone knows what made me fall for him.

We started going out, first to the park after college and then to the cinema and out to dinner now and then. Hasan's hair was like my dad's, thick and curly, and he had a warm smile.

Arif told me it was better to keep my distance and I, being stubborn, refused to listen. Arif was only jealous, he couldn't tolerate competition. Not that I was interested in him. I didn't care what Arif thought. But the thing that did worry me was what would happen if Uncle Naveed found out about my friendship with Hasan. The only person wicked enough to tell him was Arif. I had no choice but to grovel to him and ask him not to spill the beans.

That guy wasn't one to make life easy for me. He was in one of his sulky moods. 'So what's wonder-boy up to these days? Has he decided whether or not he's going to be the next man on the moon?'

He was so sarcastic at times!

'Don't try to be funny Arif, it doesn't suit you. Listen there's....'

'No, you listen!' he interrupted rudely. 'What do you see in the guy? He's such a loser!'

'At least he doesn't talk about people behind their backs. What's your problem, Arif?'

'Nowt! You're mad, Stacey. He'll kick you in the teeth. Wait and see.'

'Quit talking bull,' I fumed, 'You'd better not tell your dad about Hasan.'

Arif's eyes lit up. 'Thanks for the ammunition, dear cousin. The thought hadn't even crossed my mind.'

'Just watch your mouth,' I jabbed a finger in his chest. 'If your dad finds out, I'm history.'

'I'll think about it. If I were you, I'd be careful. That Hasans's a bit of a Romeo.'

'Don't talk wet! He's nothing of the sort.'

'Suit yourself. If you don't want to listen, then that's your problem. It'll be fun saying I told you so.'

'You're jealous, aren't you?'

He shook his head adamantly. 'Don't kid yourself, Stacey. You're not my sort.'

I left his house with that edgy feeling that makes you guilty even when there's nothing wrong.

Funnily enough, my relationship with Hasan took a turn in the wrong direction. I couldn't work out what was wrong. One minute everything was brilliant and the next, it was awful.

Hasan began to behave strangely. He was moody and aggressive and things finally came to a head when he started breaking off dates. I decided it was time to confront him. He was in the college canteen sitting with a dark scowl on his face.

'Smile, it might never happen!' I said as I sat down. 'What's up, Hasan?'

'Who said anything was up?'

'Pardon me for speaking. There's no need for you to jump down my throat.'

'Shut up, Stacey!'

My eyes opened wide. He'd never spoken to me like that before. 'Hasan!'

'Not now, Stacey. I'm trying to think.'

'Well, don't try too hard,' I snapped bitchily. 'You might tire yourself out.'

'Stacey, I'm not in the mood for this right now. Can we talk later?'

'Not really. I might not feel like it later. I want to know why you didn't show last night. I waited for over an hour outside the night-club.'

'I forgot,' he looked straight at me. He seemed like a stranger.

'Have you found somebody else, Hasan?'

'Don't be silly.'

'Tell you what, Mum would like to meet you. Why don't you come round tonight?'

'Yeah, alright. I'll see you at seven.'

Shoving back his chair, he got up and walked off. Who the hell did he think he was? He had no right to put me on hold whenever he had a problem. Arif, it seemed, was right after all. Hasan wasn't the knight in shining armour I'd made him into. The rest of my day passed slowly.

By seven o'clock, I was a bloody nervous wreck. Would Mum like Hasan? How would he react when he met her? I was thinking all sorts of silly thoughts.

Mum welcomed Hasan with a warm smile and a hand-shake. He looked very attractive in his black trousers and loose white shirt. He smiled at me, sat down on the couch and tried to relax. He was tense, I could tell from the way he carried himself.

By eight o' clock, Mum and Hasan were firm friends. She liked him and that was all that mattered to me. The front door slammed. Granddad was back from the pub. He came into the room, stopped and stared at us in surprise.

Mum spoke. 'Dad, this is Hasan. He's Stacey's boyfriend.'

Granddad's eyes almost popped out of his head. 'Stacey's what?'

Hasan shuffled in his seat.

'You heard Mum,' I answered.

Granddad glared at me. His face was turning an angry red and his blue eyes glinted like polished glass. 'I don't believe this is happening,' he hissed. 'How dare you bring that,' - he pointed a crooked finger at Hasan - 'into my house?'

Mum stood up. 'Dad, there's no need to be so rude.' She tried to lead him out of the room.

Wrenching his arm free, he bellowed, 'I'm not going to stand by and watch you encourage her, Carla. I let you ruin your life. My granddaughter's not going to hang about with a Paki!'

'Now you just hold on!' Hasan got up. 'What the hell is all this about?'

'You get out!' sneered Granddad. 'Go on, sling your hook!' His body

14

shook with rage. 'I don't want your sort coming into this house.'

'Hasan's my guest,' I shouted. 'You leave him alone.'

Granddad shook his head. 'No, no, my girl. You aren't following in your mothers' footsteps. Over my dead body!'

'Don't tempt me.' I said. 'I'll see Hasan whenever I choose and you're not going to stop me.' I felt so ashamed. My family were a pain in the rear.

Hasan was incredulous. 'I don't have to put up with this sort of treatment. I'm leaving.'

'No! Hasan, please. Don't let him scare you off.'

'You've got to be joking! I'm going because I don't want to make trouble. I'll see you around.'

I watched helplessly as he walked off. I didn't have the energy to run after him.

Granddad said, 'He'll not be back, you mark my words.'

'I hate you,' I screamed. 'How could you do that to me?'

'Get up to your room and stay there until you've calmed down.'

He was such a bastard! Brushing past him, I ran up to my bedroom.

Mum came to check. She put an arm around my shoulder and tried to comfort me. 'Don't let him get to you love, I know he can be awkward.'

'Hasan's never going to talk to me again! Granddad had no right to interfere.'

'I'm sorry, Stacey. You'll have to entertain Hasan somewhere else. When I was seeing your dad all those years ago your granddad did the same thing to me. He tried to live my life for me. It's very difficult to put up with his narrow-minded views, but you'll have to try.'

'I've tried Mum. It's no good. Granddad's had it in for me from the start. I'm not going to bend over backwards to please him. I like Hasan. Why did he have to interfere?'

Mum tucked a strand of hair behind my ear. 'Come on, love. Cheer up. If you like we can go out and buy fish and chips for tea.' Sighing heavily, she added. 'Your dad loved chapati and chips.'

I cried even more as memories of Dad came back to me.

I was so annoyed with Granddad. Every time I set eyes on him, I had to stop myself kicking him in the head. What he needed was a good fist in the gob. A few days of him out of action was my idea of bliss.

Hasan gave me the cold shoulder the following day in college.

'Hi,' I said feebly.

He ignored me.

A fierce sort of anger rose inside me. 'Hey remember me, your girlfriend? What's wrong with you?'

He slammed his fist against the wall and shouted. 'You are. How dare you let him humiliate me? Nobody's ever spoken to me like that before. I don't have to put up with the kind of crap your granddad shovelled me yesterday!'

Hasan was upset.

'He's an old fool. Don't let him get to you. Granddad's not important to me. You are.'

'Nobody talks to me like that and gets away with it,' he sneered.

'Sorry, Hasan. I had no idea he was going to show up and say what he said to you.'

What the hell did he want from me? I was almost down on my knees begging him to forget everything that had happened. I couldn't believe he was such a tough nut to crack. What had happened to the guy I'd been attracted to?

'I've got a class in five minutes,' he informed me, matter of factly.

'See you at lunchtime,' I said hopefully.

'I'll be busy.'

'Hasan, why are you doing this to me?'

'I'm not going to stand here all morning and argue with you,' he snapped. 'Look, Stacey, I think it's time to call it quits.'

'What?' I asked in disbelief. 'I didn't know you were so easily put off. Why can't we talk about this in a sensible manner?'

'There's something I've been meaning to tell you. I've just never had the time to say it.' He ran his fingers through his hair. 'Stacey, there's no easy way to say this. I'm sorry. I've met someone else.'

There, it was out! Strangely enough, I wasn't as shocked as I'd thought. There was no point in trying to hang on. 'Fine, I hope you'll be very happy,' I managed.

That was a bloody lame parting shot. What I really wanted to do was slap his face. He'd gone cold on me ages ago. The mystery was solved.

'Aren't you going to say anything else?' he asked.

'If you're expecting tears and confessions of love, Hasan, you're looking at the wrong girl. I'm not into all that mushy stuff. We had a good time and that's it. End of story!'

'Is that all I was? Just a good time?'

'Yeah, that's all. If you cared about me at all, you'd have told me yonks ago you wanted out.' I wanted to make him feel low, it would be good to send him packing with a guilty conscience. 'You were seeing another girl behind my back. What does that make you, Hasan? A two-timing snake!'

He looked sheepish. 'I didn't mean to hurt you.'

'Ha, don't make me laugh! There are plenty more sleaze-balls like you around, Hasan. You were expecting me to fall at your feet in a dead faint. Well, forget it.That's not my style!'

His jaw almost hit the floor. I knew what sort of a person he was. Arif had warned me and Granddad had done me a favour in a weird way. I can't stand people who mess me about. I was rid of a bad apple and felt no sorrow at all as I left him standing rooted to the spot.

It was now time to forget about relationships. I wasn't very good at falling in love. I had bigger fish to fry. Granddad had a favourite armchair. The one in front of the fire with a good view of the television. He didn't let anybody sit in it. It seemed as though there was a reserved sign stuck on it even when he wasn't around. That chair provoked me. I wanted to show Granddad that I wasn't afraid to sit down and relax in a chair my dad had bought and he'd claimed as his own!

We'd just finished supper. Mum had retired with a Mills and Boon and Granddad had gone to take out his false teeth. There was a documentary about drugs I wanted to see. I switched on the television, sat down and waited. I was desperate to make trouble - it had been a while since we'd been at each other's throats.

Granddad let his presence be known by coughing loudly.

Drop dead, you piece of dog crap, I said to myself.

'I want to sit down,' he said impatiently as he stood by the chair.

He hated being ignored so I didn't speak to him. 'Shift yourself, girl.'

He was so bloody rude. His voice got on my nerves. Knowing that it wouldn't take long for him to get hot under the collar, I crossed my arms and sat back, my eyes fixed firmly on the television.

'Are you deaf?' he hollered.

'No, I'm not,' I replied smugly. 'What do you want?'

'Don't you speak to me in that tone of voice,' he growled.

Things were heating up now.

'Granddad, I'm watching the telly, if you don't mind I'd rather not talk.' It was fun to observe him losing his cool, not that he had much of that.

'I'm not your granddad. You're no relation of mine.'

I glared at him. 'If I recall correctly, yesterday you claimed I was your granddaughter. You must be going senile in your old age.'

'How dare you?' he asked. 'How dare you say such a thing to me?'

'I'm only stating a fact! You spoke to Hasan like he was trash. He didn't like that at all. If I were you, Granddad, I'd watch my step. He's got mates who could put you underground permanently.'

'Why, you cheeky little monkey! Are you trying to threaten me? His face had blanched.

'Would I do something like that?' I asked innocently. 'Go lie down, Granddad, you're in the way.'

That really upset him, he looked like an overheated bull. 'You just wait,' he fumed before leaving the room. 'Carla,' he yelled, 'Carla, get down here now!'

'You leave Mum out of this. She's not a puppet on a string who's going to bloody dance every time you clap your hands.'

He was in such a rage. 'I warned her this would happen, but she refused to listen to me. Multi-coloured kids with no manners and no respect. She married trash and she gave birth to trash.'

'Don't you dare call my dad trash. He was a better man than you'll ever be.' I was so mad at him, my eyes were watering.

'You cheeky little ape,' he grumbled. 'I warned her but would she listen to me? Oh no! She insisted on doing things her own way. Well, I'm not letting history repeat itself.'

'You aren't going to run my life for me, you stupid old fool. I'm going to do exactly what I like.'

Spluttering loudly, he shook his fist at me. 'Don't give me none of your lip. I'll box your ears for you.'

'Just try it! I swear I'll report you if you so much as touch me!'

My head was pounding with fury. I wanted to fist him one.

Mum came downstairs. 'What on earth is going on?'

Usually, I don't go running to Mum with tales, but this time was an exception. 'He started it, Mum, he wants a fight and if he's not careful, he'll get one.'

'Calm down, Stacey,' Mum came into the room. 'Dad, what's all this about?'

Granddad grumbled but didn't say anything intelligible.

'Well!' She had her hands on her hips and looked annoyed at being dragged out of bed to sort out another argument. 'You know I have to be up early for work. What's going on?'

'He called Dad trash. He said that you wouldn't listen to him and that I was multi-coloured.'

Mum was shocked. 'Dad, did you say that?'

'Don't listen to her, Carla. She's telling lies.' A red flush crept across Granddad's face. 'She's out to make trouble as usual,' he sneered.

Mum sighed helplessly. 'I'm not in the mood to defend either of you. Dad, you've got to stop picking on Stacey.'

'Don't tell me what to do, girl,' he said, 'I'm your father and you'd better watch your manners.'

Mum wasn't going to let him scare her off. 'For the sake of peace, Dad, just stop making life unbearable around here. And you, Stacey, get upstairs and watch the telly in your room. I'm sick to death of being the referee in your wrestling matches. Go on, Stacey, get moving!'

Sticking my tongue out at Granddad, I hurried out of the room. As I got ready for bed, I went over everything that had happened. Granddad really despised me and he made no excuses for the way he felt either. I threw my socks into a corner of the room and climbed into bed, pulling the duvet over my head.

Mum walked past my room, the floorboard in the landing groaned as she stepped on it. I'd never seen her so mad at Granddad before. She's a peace-loving sort of person who minds her own business. For the first time in my life, I'd witnessed some backlash from her. That meant there was still room for hope. I fell asleep with a sense of relief I'd never experienced before.

The air was frosty in our dining room when I got down to breakfast. Granddad was sulking over his bowl of cornflakes.

Mum placed a cup of coffee in front of me. 'You're going to be late for college.'

'I'm not going in.'

'Why not?'

'Don't feel like it. I can't face Hasan.'

Mum sighed heavily. 'You can't hide from him. You'll have to go to college whether you like it or not.'

'Mum, stop nagging and leave me alone!'

'Don't talk to your mother like that,' Granddad butted in.

'Who rattled your cage?'

'Stacey,' Mum said,'stop it, please.'

'You tell him to back off. Why can't he keep his nose out of my business?'

Granddad got to his feet. 'I see I'm not wanted around here. I'll take myself off somewhere else.'

'You do that!' I said angrily.

Mum was caught up in the middle of a battlefield. 'Stacey, Dad. Please, both of you, stop this foolishness.'

Granddad had to get the weight off his chest. 'This is what comes of doing your own thing. If you'd listened to me all them years ago, she wouldn't be here today talking to me in such a brazen manner. You mark my words, Carla, she'll break your heart!'

Mum covered her face with her hands. 'I've had it with both of you,' her voice was muffled. 'I'm fed up! Why can't you leave each other alone?'

'I'm going out so don't bother waiting for me. I might not be coming back.' I announced.

Mum stared at me with a look on helpless look on her face that said, where the hell did I go wrong with her?

That night I stayed at Uncle Naveed's house. All he said was, 'Another argument with your granddad?'

I informed him I needed some breathing space out of Granddad's way. Uncle Naveed didn't question me. He'd helped us rebuild our lives after Dad had died. Never in all those years had he turned us away.

My cousin Sameena gave me a warm welcome. She was cleaning out her bedroom which she claimed was a dump. I tell you it was a hell of a lot neater than mine.

Her single bed was tucked snugly underneath the window. The sill was cluttered with a strange assortment of fluffy toys. A large red rug covered the carpet.

Sameena was polishing the dressing-table mirror with a duster. 'It gets so filthy in here,' she told me as I flopped down on her bed. 'I like it when it's tidy.'

'Relax, Sammy. Don't kill yourself. It looks fine to me. You should see mine. It looks like Granddad's been breaking wind in it. All my clothes are stuck to the bleeding ceiling.'

'Are you stopping over, Stacey?'

'Yeah, if you don't mind me kipping on the floor.'

'What's wrong with the spare room?' she asked.

'Nowt. Thought you'd prefer my company tonight.'

'I could do with someone else to talk to. Arif's got his head stuck up in the clouds at the moment. Don't say anything but he's got a girlfriend.'

I pulled a face. 'Poor cow! Who is she?'

Sameena shrugged. 'Don't know. I just happened to run into them in town today. She's quite pretty.'

'I split with Hasan.'

Sameena was all ears. Tossing the duster aside, she sat down and said, 'Tell me more.'

I quickly related all the events of the past few days to her. She was a good listener and I felt a lot better for talking to her. When I'd finished telling my tale, she said, 'I'm sorry, Stacey, but these things do happen.'

'I was really shocked at the time. But now, if I'm honest with you, Sammy, I'm glad it's over and done with. Hasan was looking at me like I'd sprouted two heads. I wanted to hit him!'

'Guys aren't to be trusted if you ask me. How come men think they're better than us?'

'Because their mothers told them that they'd grow up nice and strong if they ate all their greens, ' I said sarcastically. 'They haven't got the bloody sense they were born with. They do nowt but think through their trousers!'

Sameena chuckled. 'Sounds like you're fed up with the opposite sex. Give it time, you'll get over it.'

'If I had my way, all the men on this planet would have been drowned at birth, Granddad first, then the rest in dribs and drabs.'

We talked late into the night, often bursting into loud fits of laughter. Uncle Naveed banged on the door to quieten us down. But Sameena had some problems which she needed to confide in me. She was due to travel to Pakistan in the summer where she had to get married. The idea didn't please her at all. She'd looked quite ferocious at the prospect of leaving Bradford behind.

We both knew that Uncle Naveed wouldn't relax until Sameena was out of the country. I found myself feeling sorry for her. All the arrangements for the wedding had been made. Sameena hadn't been consulted about anything. She was merely a pawn in another one of Uncle Naveed's schemes. All my life I'd been thinking that I'd got it tough. Only when Sameena told me how she felt did I realise just how lucky I really was.

Uncle Naveed was getting into his car when I walked up the road to our house. My heart skipped a beat. He looked so much like Dad, same hair, same walk. I waved at him and went into the house.

Mum called from the kitchen. 'Stacey, that you?'

I was still pissed off with her and Granddad but decided not to start another fight. She was peeling potatoes. I plonked myself down at the table and told her I'd seen Uncle Naveed. Mum informed me he'd been round and had told her that Sameena was going to Pakistan.

He'd also wanted to know if I was willing to marry Arif.

My God! That really threw me. They were mad if they thought I was sick enough to marry that moron. Mum was so dense at times. How could she even think about something so ridiculous? I really shouldn't have been surprised. It was Uncle Naveed's idea and Mum, as usual, was willing to go along with him. She was so easily manipulated.

She wasn't very happy when I refused to go along with the idea of marrying a total idiot. Arif and I had been fighting each other since the cradle.

Mum didn't understand how I felt. I'd just split with Hasan, I needed time to get over the way he'd betrayed me. Apart from all that, I wasn't ready to settle down. I had my wild oats to sow and marriage was a step in the wrong direction as far as I was concerned.

I think the idea of me in a wedding dress appealed to Mum. She was romantic and that dreamy look on her face made me uncomfortable. Mum had wanted a daughter who liked frocks and frills, instead she'd ended up with a tear-away, loud-mouthed tomboy. Trying my best to explain to her I wasn't interested was a waste of time. She used Sameena as an example. That made me sick! Parents always compare you with your friends or the daughters of their own friends. And Mum liked Sameena very much.

Without thinking, I told her that Sameena didn't have a choice. She was being forced into an arranged marriage. Mum didn't believe me. I was being silly. Didn't I know Uncle Naveed would never push his kids into something that made them unhappy? She wanted me to think about it. I hate situations where I'm expected to react straightaway. It was very frustrating. There was nothing to think about.

I studied Mum's face as she worked. It was far too pale. I couldn't remember the last time I'd seen her wearing any make-up. She was so plain, her clothes were out of fashion by about a century. And she was wearing the ugliest cardigan she owned. When Dad had been around, Mum had looked fabulous. But since he'd died, she'd really let herself go. These days, all she did was go to work, come home in the evenings, cook supper and then go up to her bedroom. She led a very boring life and didn't even know it. She never went for a night out with friends and nobody came around to our house to see her.

When Mum wanted her own way she always told me Uncle Naveed had done a lot for us. That was meant to make me feel appreciative. Well, it didn't always work! It didn't mean I had got to lick his boots and trot off like a lamb to the slaughter every time he clapped his hands!

Mum said, 'Calm down, Stacey.'

'Arif's a conceited idiot and I can't stand him.'

'You're very selfish.'

My eyes widened in disbelief. 'I'm selfish?' I squeaked. 'You're calling me selfish? I can't believe we're having such a stupid conversation.' Putting on a brave face was difficult. My voice shook with emotion.

'Stop being so dramatic,' Mum bit out, 'Arif's a good boy. I'm sure that your dad would've wanted you to do it.'

That really was the final straw! There was no way she was going to drag Dad into such a ridiculous plan.

'Don't use emotional blackmail on me, Mum. I know for a fact Dad would never have forced me into a corner like you're trying to.' I paused for a moment to catch my breath. 'You're trying to get rid of me again. Well, I won't let you, Mum. This is my house too and I've got every right to be here. I'm not about to walk out and let you and Granddad have the last laugh.'

After Dad's death Mum'd packed me off for a few weeks. Sure, Uncle Naveed and Aunt Razia had taken good care of me. They'd treated me like one of their own. But Mum should have been there for me. She'd let Granddad bully her into getting rid of me and, for a while, he got what he wanted. My Mum all to himself.

Mum looked as though she'd been slapped. Her lips trembled slightly. Then, without speaking she left the kitchen. A sharp twinge of guilt surged through my body. I hated getting on the wrong side of her.

There was no place in particular where I had to be, so I went into the city centre to calm down. John Street Market with its menagerie of stalls and shops was my favourite place. I headed there. The familiar sights and smells helped me relax. My stomach grumbled noisily. I bought myself a can of coke and a bag of chips. I was walking past the sweet stall when I bumped into the root of all my troubles. Arif!

'Hey, Stacey,' he said dipping his hand into my chips, 'how you doing?'

The urge to ignore him was overpowering, but he was bloody greeting me as if I'd just returned from the moon.

He grinned and said, 'Say something, woman! Fancy going to the photography museum with me?'

'I'd rather jump under a bus,' I informed him and continued walking.

'Come on, Stacey, don't be so nasty. Hey, I heard you and what's his face split up. Told you it'd never last, didn't I?'

'Mind your own business, Arif.'

'Tell me what happened. Did he do the dumping or was it you?'

'Get lost. People are staring at us.'

'Let them, Stacey, spill the beans! I'm dying to know what went wrong.'

'I'm not telling you!'

'If it was me who'd split up with some bird,' he added generously, 'I'd tell you everything.'

'What makes you think I'd care to know? You never even told me you had a girlfriend.'

'That's because you never asked me,' he stated arrogantly. 'Anyway, you keep quiet about that. If Dad finds out, that's me done for!'

There'd been a time when I'd said very much the same thing to him about Hasan and he'd made me sweat. 'I've a good mind to tell him. He has a right to know what his idiot son's up to behind his back.'

'Don't, Stacey. I'm not that keen on Kashmir. I might finish with her now you're available.'

Shaking my head slowly, I said, 'You really are sick in the head. If you were the last guy on this bloody planet, I'd take my own life!'

'That's what I like about you,' he admitted, 'you always say no when you really mean yes! Relax, honey, I'm not going to eat you!'

'Don't call me honey,' I seethed.

'What would you like me to call my future wife?' he asked boldly.

'What the hell are you babbling about?'I screamed. 'You're mad!'

'You and me baby,' he gestured dramatically, 'Husband and wife.'

The idea seemed to please him. He beamed from ear to ear. I was reminded of a droning fly which kept returning for another swatting. Arif was walking on very thin ice.

I could feel my face bright red as I snapped at him, 'For the love of God, stop messing about! You've got rocks in your head.'

'Come on, hon', lighten up!' He tried to put his arm around me.

I shoved him away. 'You've got another think coming if you imagine I'm going to marry you,' I replied. 'I haven't lost my marbles just yet and anyway, you're involved with someone else.'

'You,' he informed me as he tweaked my cheek, 'are a woman. My woman.'

'Piss off!'

'Tut, tut, dear cousin. Where on earth did you inherit such a foul temper from? No, don't tell me. Let me guess.' He clicked his fingers very loud. 'Ha, I know! From your granddad Arthur, the little shit. So how are you two getting along these days?'

'Why don't you f......'

'Now, now, Stacey, temper temper. Language like that will get you into big trouble. I'm really looking forward to the day when I'll have the pleasure of bringing you to your knees.'

Reaching out, I slapped him across his clean-shaven face. He looked startled. Then, all of a sudden, a lazy smile stretched across his face.

That was one thing that really annoyed me about Arif. He'd rather die than admit defeat. Why couldn't he be like other people and know when it was time to quit? He seemed to bounce back no matter how many times he'd been knocked down.

'Stacey, you're so sexy! I love it when you blow your top.You're adorable.'

People were giving us weird looks so I decided to make a run for it. Pushing past Arif, I took a short cut out of the market through Morrisons. I hoped I'd shake him off. Unfortunately that didn't stop him shadowing me. It just made him all the more determined.

His voice mocked me, 'Hey baby slow down. I'm not going to eat you!'

'Leave me alone,' I looked over my shoulder at him and almost bumped into a little kid.

'Yo, prickles, what's with you?' he asked as he fell into step with me again. Arif always managed to bring out the bitch in me. I'd made up my mind to swing for him again if his pestering didn't cease.

He tapped me on the shoulder, 'It's gone one, why don't you let me buy you lunch?'

'I'm not hungry. I ate earlier.'

'Come on, baby, chill out!'

He wouldn't leave me alone. I felt like screaming until there was no more breath left in my body. I stopped abruptly, and turned to face him.

'What's wrong with you? You're always so bloody miserable.'

I jabbed a finger in his chest. 'Leave me alone, otherwise you'll end up with a black eye!'

He held up his hands in a defeated manner. 'I really can't figure you out. I'm being honest when I say I find you attractive, but that's not the only reason I'm always tailing you. I want to be mates with you. But you can't hack that, so go to hell!'

Then he marched off. His confession threw me a little. I'd never have been able to open up about my feelings like that. He'd offered me his friendship and I'd thrown it back in his face. I could always apologise to him later on but the thought of having to grovel made me feel uneasy. I hated situations which left me open to attack from outsiders.

I didn't know what I wanted. I was torn both ways. Part of me longed for some security and happiness. Did that mean I'd find it in a relationship with Arif? I could never be guaranteed of having everything I desired. The rebel in my nature wanted a bit of fun, a life that was totally different to my mum's. I couldn't bear to be like her. All she did was exist. Life was like the housework for her. It had to be done and there was no time for any laughs along the way. I had to get away from home before my family ruined me!

The more I thought about it, the more attractive the idea became. I made all sorts of wonderful plans. Wild parties, late nights out with mates. I'd be able to do exactly what I wanted and I'd never have to answer to Mum or anyone else.

Angry voices were lifting the roof off our house when I got home. Granddad was shouting fit to bust. I crept into the hallway, stood behind the door and listened to what he was saying. 'No granddaughter of mine's going to marry a Paki! Over my dead body! How dare you suggest such a bloody stupid thing?'

My heart missed a beat, it was amazing how I became his relation when he wanted his own way. My time for revenge had finally arrived. Let him suffer. He'd given me enough trouble over the years.

Mum murmured something I didn't hear.

Then Uncle Naveed spoke. 'Stacey is my niece. Her father would have wanted this so let's not argue.'

'Don't you give me that bloody rubbish!' roared Granddad. 'Who the hell do you think you are? Carla threw her life away on a Paki. I was too late to stop her. This time things'll go my way. That girl isn't marrying a stinking Paki.'

He was very sure of himself. I was prepared to do anything he disapproved of. If marrying Arif was a bad thing in his eyes, then that was what I'd do. Pushing open the door, I stepped inside. Granddad was pacing the floor. He had a savage look in his piggy, blue eyes. Uncle

Naveed stood by the window and Mum had perched herself on the arm of the couch.

Granddad caught sight of me and scowled. 'There you are girl, come on in and shut the door behind you.'

He spoke to me like I was drosh. I'd just about had enough of his insults. I remained where I was.

'Are you deaf lass? Do as you're told!'

I snapped angrily. 'Don't order me about. I'm not a little kid.'

His head shot up. 'What was that?'

'You heard me the first time,' I retorted.

'Of all the cheek,' he spluttered, showering the carpet with a spray of spit. The filthy devil, he looked so ugly with his eyes almost popping out of their sockets. He decided to pick on Mum. 'You see, Carla, if you hadn't married that Paki, you wouldn't be worrying yourself stupid because of her. She's a cheeky monkey!'

Cruel bastard! Mum looked ready to cry. He'd always managed to make her feel small and helpless. I knew that Mum wouldn't say anything to contradict him. I shook and I screamed, 'What the hell do you want from us? You miserable sod!'

'Stacey,' Mum said. 'Don't talk to your granddad like that.'

'How can you take his side? All he ever does is have a go at Dad and you never object. If you can't defend Dad, then you leave me with no other choice, Mum. I'll have to do your dirty work for you.' A mixture of anger and self pity made me lose my temper. There was nobody on my side. Would I have to fight Granddad alone? Why wouldn't Mum help me? She seemed to cringe at the thought of another quarrel. She was nothing but a coward!

Uncle Naveed spoke to me. 'Calm down, Stacey. There's no need to get so carried away.'

'You're as bad as them. Dad was your brother! Where's your family loyalty gone? Does he frighten you?' I pointed an accusing finger in Granddad's direction.

Uncle Naveed shook his head and said, 'I'm not afraid, Stacey. I'm not going to stoop as low as your granddad.'

Granddad glared at him. 'You've got no right to come into our house with your stupid ideas. Go on, get out.'

He enjoyed chucking people out of our house. Just because he was as old as the hills, didn't mean he was the boss! He seemed to think he could bully everybody. Granddad didn't like Uncle Naveed. To be honest, he didn't like anybody. He was so patronising and arrogant. Well, he wasn't going to get away with it this time.

'You've never had anything nice to say about my family. You were threatened by Dad because he put you in your place. This house belonged to him, he bought it and that means you've got no claim to it!' I was on a high and there was no way I was coming down until I'd had my kicks. How I longed to tell him what I thought of him. He'd never treated me like I was his granddaughter. He'd always made me feel guilty for being in the way. He only had to clap his hands and Mum was at his beck and call. The guy was selfish and mean.

'You're a meddling old fool and I hate you!'

Mum stood up. 'Stacey, that's enough.'

She didn't want me to say anything, I could tell from the way she threw me that begging look.

I happened to glance at Uncle Naveed. The poor man was trying very hard to keep a straight face. The only person who wasn't amused was the old git.

'Shut your mouth, you saucy little tart!'

My mouth fell open. Nobody had ever called me such a charming name before.

Uncle Naveed stepped in. 'There is no need to use such language.'

'Get lost,' bellowed Granddad, 'This is a conspiracy, you and her always siding with each other!'

The argument was heating up! Granddad had sworn at me and Mum hadn't objected. That was typical of her. As long as she didn't get into trouble, she didn't give a bloody shit about my feelings!

Uncle Naveed walked out of the room.

Running after him, I caught hold of his arm. 'Don't go. You can't leave me here to fight him on my own.'

He spoke kindly. 'I'm not staying where I'm not welcome.' He turned to Mum. 'Carla, it's up to you to sort out this mess.'

'Go on, sling your hook!' Granddad hissed. He shot Uncle Naveed a contemptuous look.

'He's not going anywhere,' I stated, 'So stop giving orders. Come on, Uncle Naveed.'

He seemed to think about it and then, thankfully, decided to stay.

Granddad seized me viciously by the arm, his bony fingers dug into my flesh. All the hair on my body stood on end.

'Any more of your lip and you'll get a thick ear,' he snarled, 'I'm sick of you!'

I clenched my teeth. 'Get your hands off me. You touch me again and I'll swing for you.' I managed to free myself from his vice-like grip and moved behind Uncle Naveed. From this safe place I was able to insult him and he couldn't reach me.

He almost had a stroke when I called him 'Arthur'. I insisted the word Granddad hadn't been made for a brute like him. His face was like a red balloon. 'And as far as marriage is concerned, I'll decide whether or not Arif is a suitable partner for me.'

'You'll not marry that boy!' he roared. He stepped closer. His fists were clenched so tight that the knuckles showed white. 'In my house you'll do as I say!'

I had to set the record straight, the old fool was living in cloud cuckoo land. 'You lived in that dingy, little room over the top of a shop and thought that the sun shone out of your backside, remember? I'll live my life the way I see fit. If you don't like that, then that's tough!'

He looked jumpy. 'Carla, you talk to her,' he ordered Mum, 'make her listen! She's going to give us a bad name.'

'Stuff your name up a turkey!' I said rudely.

Mum, as usual, was ready to take his side. That made me fume. I was her flesh and blood and she could only think about keeping her old dad happy. She told me to apologise. When I refused, Granddad said I was an ungrateful brat. What the hell did I have to be grateful about? If he'd had his way, I'd have grown up in a home.

Uncle Naveed didn't like the way Granddad kept calling me a troublemaker. He told him point blank he was the only person out to make trouble and that he wouldn't be insulted by him any more.

That made Granddad say some pretty terrible things. 'I've had a gutful of your bleeding family,' he thundered, 'traipsing in and out of here whenever you feel like it. This isn't a hotel! The sooner you leave and take that baggage with you,' he pointed at me,'the better!'

Uncle Naveed was far too polite to yell back and Mum was afraid of him. He only had to glare at her and off she'd skitter like a frightened rabbit.

'Dad, come on, don't be silly!' Mum said.

'I'm not being silly, you foolish woman. She'll put us all to shame.'

Enough was enough. I had to get out. There was no way on earth Granddad would ever treat me like a human being. He'd always see me as some sort of genetic accident. 'I'm moving out today,' I said, feeling amazingly calm. 'You can have this place to yourself now.'

Everybody stared at me. Mum was pale, she had dark smudges under her eyes and her mousy brown hair dangled untidily about her face. 'Where will you go?'

'I'll stay with Uncle Naveed.'

Uncle Naveed's eyebrows shot upwards. The look on his rugged face said clearly, 'Thanks for dropping me in it, Stacey.'

'Is that okay with you?' I prayed he wouldn't reject me when I was depending on him to help me out.

He nodded silently.

'Good, let's go then.'

'Carla, stop her,' Granddad whined. 'If you let her walk out, there's no telling what she might do.'

I couldn't figure him out. First, he wanted me out of the way and when I was ready to leave, he wanted Mum to stop me. The man was afraid of my not having to turn to Mum and him for help. Not that I ever did! 'Count your blessings, Arthur. I'll be out of your bald patch by the end of the day.'

He was grey with annoyance. A muscle twitched in his jaw, his false teeth made a horrid clicking sound as he ground them together.

Mum tried to stop me. I'd have stayed, but the fact that she never stood by me made me feel resentful. Every time I'd turned to her, she'd pushed me away. I couldn't take any more of being second best. Uncle Naveed followed me out of the room. Behind me, I could hear Mum crying. I felt sorry for her until I heard Granddad growl, 'Let her go, Carla. Didn't I tell you she'd break your heart?'

31

Living with Uncle Naveed and his family was just what I needed. They accepted me the way I was, with my torn jeans and long shirts, with my loud voice and stubbornness. For them, I didn't have to make any excuses. There was no need to pretend I was any different. It didn't need much to make them happy and the fact I'd chosen to live with them cheered Sameena up.

She was a lively girl, full of energy and a zest for life that many people lacked. So much had happened over such a short period of time, the pain of being ditched by Hasan had gone, the rejection that had always upset me didn't bother me anymore. I felt more relaxed. Even Arif had stopped pestering me. Once he'd insisted I accompany him and Kashmir on an outing to the seaside. I'm sure nobody'd told him two was company and a third person would be like finding a bone in a kebab.

Sameena said he was a kid with a new toy and once the novelty wore off, he'd leave me alone. She was right. Sharing the same house had the desired effect. He soon began to see me as a sister rather than a potential girlfriend.

During the day I went to college, and in the evenings Sameena and I would mess about with make-up and read magazines. I also liked spending the weekend with Aunt Razia. She was teaching me how to make round chapatis. Mine always looked like they'd had a fight on the way to the cooker.

Three months elapsed. In all that time I'd seen Mum twice, once in town and once when she'd come to visit me at Uncle Naveed's. On both occasions, she'd asked me to return home. I'd told her I wasn't ready, that I needed more time. I didn't want her to be under the impression I'd forgotten her. Things had been blown out of all proportion.

Granddad had managed to turn the tables on me again. I couldn't stand him managing to have the last word. I'd have given anything to be rid of him for good.

It was a miserable grey day, the kind that made me want to stay in bed. Rain trickled down the pane of glass in a steady stream. Arif and Uncle Naveed had left early in the morning to collect a new supply of material from Birmingham. Uncle Naveed sold it and when the stock was low, he had to go and buy more. He'd tried to tempt me many times with the beautiful rolls of material on display in the shop on Whetley Lane. 'Make yourself a nice suit, Stacey. This blue colour will look very good on you.' He didn't know I couldn't sew.

Aunt Razia was humming a tune to herself as she pottered around the kitchen. Sameena had gone out shopping. The rain had put me off accompanying her.

After a hot shower and a change of clothes, I asked Aunt Razia if it was okay to use the 'phone. Giving me one of her bright smiles, she told me to go ahead. The 'phone was engaged. Replacing the receiver, I sat down on the bottom step and waited. I tried again. The 'phone rang. 'Hi, Mum. It's me, Stacey,' I said eagerly.

A male voice answered, 'Can you hold the line? I'll go and get her for you, she's in the bedroom.'

What was going on? My hand shook slightly as I waited for Mum to come to the 'phone.

'Stacey, hello, love.'

'Mum, who was that?'

'Just a friend. Are you okay, love?'

'Yeah. What about you?'

'Couldn't be better. Look, love. I'm a bit pushed for time. Can you call back later?'

'Well....erm....yeah, sure.'

'Bye, then, love.'

The click of the 'phone and the buzzing tone told me all I needed to know. Mum had been brief. I wanted to know what she was up to. She hadn't asked me to come home and the way she'd rushed me made me feel she didn't really care any more.

Retracing my steps to the kitchen, I sat down. Aunt Razia wanted to know if I'd spoken to Mum. I sure as hell had done that. Talk about the shortest 'phone call ever made! It took longer to dial the bloody number. My mind raced. Who was the mystery man and why had Mum been so evasive? I took the washing out of the machine for Aunt Razia and folded it.

'What is the matter, Stacey?'

'It's Mum. She had a man in the house with her.'

She laughed softly. 'Look at your face in the mirror. You look as if you will explode.'

'Something's going on. Mum was dying to get rid of me.'

'Do not be silly, your mother loves you, you know that. The man could have been a friend of your grandfather's.'

Granddad didn't have many friends. Well, not that I'd seen. He did go out to the pub now and then. Maybe he'd started inviting his mates round now I was no longer likely to show him up. I told Aunt Razia how I felt about Granddad.

She placed the lid on the pressure cooker. 'You should not be so bitter. He is your grandfather. Do not let him get the better of you.'

Put like that, it all seemed so straight-forward and simple. In reality a feud with Granddad wasn't easy to forget. 'You going to give me a lecture?' I asked.

'No, you kids are all the same. I can talk to Arif and Sameena until I am blue in the face, they never hear a word I say if it does not please them.' She wiped the table top and smiled at me.

'Nobody understands,' I stated childishly. 'When Dad died, I felt like an outcast in my own home. Granddad's always gone out of his way to make my life miserable. I wish he'd died instead of my dad!'

'Do not say that, you silly girl!' Her scolding didn't annoy me. I kept watching her as she went about her work. She peeled an orange and sliced it thinly. Next, she washed the dishes she'd used in preparing the curry.

Aunt Razia had the most beautiful almond-shaped eyes I'd ever seen. Her hair was jet-black, long and she always wore it in a plait. I liked the dimple that appeared in her right cheek when she smiled.

She opened the cupboard under the sink and took out a blue bowl. 'You are so stubborn,' she informed me as she filled it with brown flour, 'why keep up the fighting if it is so upsetting, hmm? Do you want to go home, Stacey?'

She didn't beat about the bush.

'I do and I don't. Granddad would have a field day if I went home and apologised for all the stuff I said.'

'You have to make a few sacrifices in order to get by. It is your decision. I will not tell you what to do.'

She poured water into the bowl of flour and began to mix the contents with her hand. She worked quickly and made the job look easy. When a large ball of dough had formed, she picked it up and put it on a plate. She rinsed out the bowl, put back the dough and kneaded it with her fists until it was manageable.

'Do you enjoy all of this? You seem to be so happy doing housework and caring for your family.'

Aunt Razia sighed. 'This is now a routine, Stacey. I have no time to think about anything else. My reactions are automatic.' She gazed at me. 'You are different to me. At your age, I had to accept the fact that marriage and children would be my future. My life was planned for me. I did not decide anything for myself. An education was what I wanted. But you do not need a degree to cook and clean.'

I admired Aunt Razia for her honesty. Compared to her I was a wimp! 'You should get out a bit more,' I tried to be helpful, 'go to the Women's Centre.'

'I cannot do that. Your uncle would not approve. My place is here, with my family. What are you going to do when you leave college?'

'Try to find a decent job. At least the secretarial course'll help out later. I want to go and see Mum.'

'You can go any time you like,' she said kindly. 'There is no need to worry. Your mother is not going anywhere.'

I decided not to go that very same day. I was curious but didn't want Mum to think I was snooping around. If I turned up at the house just like that, she'd know I was trying to poke my nose in where it wasn't wanted.

The next day after college, I made my way straight home. It was cold outside. My teeth chattered noisily as I hurried across the road. A green Volvo was parked outside our house, full of camping gear. On closer observation, I spotted Mum's Gladstone bag on the front driving seat. I was dying to find out what was going on. Quietly, I turned the key in the lock and crept into the hall. I felt like a bloody thief, sneaking about hoping I wouldn't get caught. I heard Mum's voice.

'Mick, hurry up. We'll be late.'

Mick! Who the hell was Mick?

I walked upstairs into my bedroom. It was easy to hear everything from there without drawing any attention to my presence. The toilet flushed and the sound of footsteps thundered down the stairs.

'Come on, love,' said Mick. 'Where's your dad?'

'He's waiting in the car. Mick, I'm so excited.'

The front door slammed.

Dashing into Mum's room, I peeped through the net curtain. Granddad sat in the back, looking quite pleased. Mick helped Mum into the car. He was a tall man with shocking ginger hair and a muscular body. I felt like throwing up! So much had happened behind my back.

Mum had even got herself a hair-cut. The long strands of mousy hair had been replaced by a healthy mop of bouncing curls. I hadn't recognised her for a moment. She'd looked happy and carefree.

The room was beginning to swim. I sat down on the bed and rocked back and forth miserably. I was all alone in the house and I didn't like it.

Mum had made a few changes. The familiar paintings of flower vases had been replaced with paintings of castles and deserts. She'd got a television set in her room.

My shock turned to anger when I discovered my dad's photograph had been swapped for a picture of ginger nut himself, grinning from ear to ear. How could she do that? She was trying to get rid of Dad's memory!

A large bottle of Lou Lou caught my eye. Mum always wore Pink Rose. The reality of what had happened hit me like a thunder bolt. Mick must have bought it for her. There was no other explanation. I kicked the paper-basket and it rolled across the floor. A half-used bottle of Pink Rose toppled out across the carpet.

Dad had loved that perfume. I picked it up and held the cool glass bottle in my clammy hands. If Mum wanted to forget Dad, that was up to her. I, on the other hand, had every intention of keeping hold of his memory. I missed him so much.

They say a good cry helps to clear your head. After I'd finished, my head felt like it had been bloody kicked! My eyes were red and swollen and my face was all puffed up. I blew my nose and stood up.

Mum'd gone off with some awful man behind my back. What kind of person would do a thing like that to their own kid? How dare she find herself a man! And he was ugly! What the hell did she see in him?

Granddad had looked smug. He must have had a hand in their liaison. That old bastard! I wanted to get him back for all the misery he'd inflicted on me over the years. I pocketed the perfume - Mum didn't want it, I figured it was okay for me to keep it.

I stormed into Granddad's room. It was neat and tidy. His tartan slippers peeped out from under the bed. An idea came to me. I went into the bathroom with them and filled the hand basin with water. Then down to the kitchen where I rummaged about in the cupboards until I found the packet of cress seeds that Mum kept for salads and sandwiches. Granddad's slippers were wet through. I pulled out the plug, wiped my hands on the towel and tore a long piece of toilet paper off the roll. With this, I lined the slippers and sprinkled a generous amount of seeds inside.

I placed them back under the bed. What a shock he'd get when he found his slippers knackered!

I searched his room for something else he cherished and found a black and white photograph of Grandma Harris. First of all, I wanted to rip it up. It'd teach him a lesson, the interfering old devil! Deciding not to be so cruel, I chucked it behind the wardrobe. Let him accuse me if he wanted to. There was no way he'd be able to point the finger of blame at me.

I sat down in Mum's room. An awful twisting pain travelled around my body. Dad's memory had finally been laid to rest in this house. I was certain Mum'd put him out of her thoughts. That realisation hurt me incredibly. Maybe I was being selfish. I couldn't imagine another bloke taking his place. My dad had played a big part in Mum's boring life! And she was bloody pretending he'd never existed!

I went back to my sanctuary. Aunt Razia commented on my paleness, I pleaded a headache and went up to the bedroom where Sameena was busy unpacking all of her shopping. It looked like she'd bought up everything in town. Flicking her hair away from her face, she showed me the new make-up and the slippers and the clothes and all the rest of the junk she claimed she needed to take with her to Pakistan. I wasn't in the mood to show enthusiasm but didn't want to hurt her feelings. So I sat back and came out with 'Nice!' and 'Brilliant' whenever she showed me something new.

All the time I couldn't help thinking about Mum and her boyfriend. In my eyes, Mum was always Mum. She didn't have a separate identity and she certainly didn't go out with men. She couldn't change. Her baggy, tasteless cardigans and drab wardrobe would remain the same forever. She hadn't even considered my feelings when she'd let Mick drive her off into the sunset. Well, two could play her sort of game! If Mum didn't want me in her life, then I meant to stay away!

A week later, Mum returned from her holiday and called to see me.

Arif let her in. 'Whoa, what a sight!' he exclaimed. 'Hey, everybody, take a look at Aunt Carla!'

Mum laughed. 'Are you going to keep me standing in the hallway all day?'

'Sorry, come on through. Stacey, your mum's here.'

Mum looked lovely. She hugged me and said, 'Hello love, how are you?'

'Fine,' I replied sullenly.

Arif butted in, 'So what gives, Aunt Carla? Don't tell me there's a man in your life.'

I swear he had a nerve. Mum flushed scarlet. I shot Arif a dirty look.

'Am I right? You look really smart and I like the hair cut. It suits you.'

'Do you think so?' She was like a silly teenager not used to compliments. She touched her hair. 'I feel good, I've been to Wales for a bit of a break.'

Arif grinned at her. They both made me feel like I was invisible. Mum was taking Arif into her confidence. That useless no-hoper was using his charm to wheedle information out of her.

'Make yourself comfortable, Aunt Carla. Our Stacey's got no manners!'

'Shut your gob!'

He laughed at me, 'Well, if you can't entertain your old mum, I might as well do it for you.'

'Hey, I'll have less of the old,' said Mum sparkling with vitality.

Arif was determined to find out everything and kept pushing Mum until she told him about Mick. She looked at me when she spoke, most probably for approval. She could get lost. I'd never give it to her now!

Granddad had taken her to the pub with him about two months ago, she hadn't been that keen to go, but he'd insisted, and she, as usual, couldn't say no. That's when she met Mick. He was drinking with a group of people Granddad knew. Once the introductions were over,

Mum and Mick got talking. They liked each other and had continued to see each other since.

I felt my jaw drop. Mum at the pub! Hell, she'd really outdone herself this time. When you loved someone as much as Mum had loved my dad, you couldn't just go off with somebody else!

I watched her as she sipped her coffee. She'd changed so much. Her eyelashes were lightly mascaraed and she wore a pale pink lipstick. As she lifted her cup, I saw the silver ring on the middle finger of her right hand. My eyes scanned her left hand, the gold wedding band had gone. I couldn't believe it! A cold sweat broke out all over my body.

'Stacey,' Mum asked, 'you okay, love?' She stood up quickly. The room was closing in around me and I felt like throwing up.

Arif spoke. 'I think she's going to faint!' His voice boomed inside my head.

I wanted to faint just to show them I could. I tried so hard I lost my concentration and the dizziness subsided.

Mum touched my arm. I flinched away.

'Don't come near me,' I hissed, 'I hate your guts!'

She recoiled in horror. I didn't look back as I ran out of the house.

My breath came out in loud gasps as I continued to run. Tears streamed down my face and my sobs were almost choking me. I only slowed down when Manningham Park beckoned. I don't know why I felt so tired, I'd been defeated and now my isolation was complete. There wasn't a single person on my side, everyone I knew was on the other side of the fence. Even Arif had been pleased for Mum. He hadn't been put off by her appearance or the news she had a boyfriend.

I walked on the grass and deliberately crushed the daffodils and crocuses in my way. Why was it so difficult for me to accept that life had to change? At one stage, I'd been so sick of Mum's pathetic behaviour. And now she'd undergone a rapid transformation which I neither liked nor wanted to accept.

I spent the rest of the day in the park watching the kids play. Their laughter and sense of fun did nothing to lift my spirits.

At seven in the evening, I went back. Uncle Naveed and Aunt Razia were out. Arif pounced on me. 'Where the hell have you been?'

'Mind your own business, you bleeding traitor.'

I tried to squeeze past him, but he blocked the way. 'Just in case you'd like to know, your mum's gone.'

'I don't give a shit! How could you encourage her? I'll never forgive you.'

He seized my arm and hauled me into the living room. His eyes flashed angrily. 'Sit down, you stupid cow! You're such a selfish bitch, do you know that?'

I stared at him. He'd never spoken to me like that before.

He glared at me scornfully. 'What you need is a good kick in the pants. How could you be so mean to your own mum? She's always done her best for you.'

'Don't you lecture me,' I screamed. 'Who the hell do you think you are?'

Arif pushed me down again. 'You move from there and you'll bloody regret it.'

I fixed my eyes on the carpet, that was bound to get under his skin.

He continued to talk bull. 'How come you always think about yourself? As long as you get what you want, you don't give a damn about anybody else.'

'That's not true!'

'Yes, it is and well you know it! You want to feel sorry for yourself, so go right ahead. Just don't drag your mum down with you. She deserves better than you're giving her.'

I'd taken enough crap for one day. 'This is between Mum and me. It's nowt to do with you. I don't have to sit here and listen to this.'

'That's where you're wrong,' he informed me arrogantly, 'your mum confided in me. She told me about the stunt you pulled with your granddad's slippers.'

Trying to keep a straight face was a struggle. 'Don't know what you're talking about.'

'Liar! You grew cress in his slippers and don't deny it!'

'So what if I did? He deserves everything he gets.'

'You're so childish. Why don't you act your age?'

'Don't patronise me, Arif! I'm sick to death of people telling me what to do.'

'Your mum has her own life to lead. She can't live under a shadow just to make you happy.'

What he said was true. I didn't know why her having a bit of fun bothered me so much. 'I'm off to bed,' I announced sulkily, 'I've had enough of you.'

'Suit yourself. Tomorrow's a new day.'

'Go to hell!'

I couldn't sleep no matter how I tried. It was impossible for me to relax. Thousands of thoughts went round and round in my head. I snuggled under the duvet and tried to think of something that would help me forget about Mum. It was useless. I gave in and stared into the darkness. Sameena's even breathing echoed in my ears. Eventually, I drifted off. When I woke up, I felt as though I hadn't slept at all.

Sameena was already up and combing her long hair in front of the mirror. She told me my mum had called round yesterday and I'd missed her which wasn't true. Sameena hadn't been informed about my disgusting behaviour.

Another week drifted by, I was bored to death. There was nothing to do now I'd left college. I felt as though my life had come to a rather abrupt halt. Mum 'phoned me several times and on each occasion I refused to speak with her.

Uncle Naveed didn't approve of such childishness and told me to patch things up. She'd been faithful to my dad for long enough and she had to get on with her own life.

I wasn't stopping her from doing that. No matter how hard I tried to get rid of my jealousy, I couldn't. There was an awful, disturbed feeling in my gut all the time and it was driving me barmy. Everybody told me to give Mum a chance. She needed my support to get things moving with Mick.

If I disapproved for too long, I knew I'd lose Mum for good. That was something I didn't want to happen.

Eating humble pie degrades you. I had to swallow the tiny scraps of my pride and admit that I was in the wrong. It took a lot of guts for me to go home and face her.

She was in the yard pegging out the clothes. If I'd been Mum, I would've given me a tough time. But she welcomed me back home with open arms and said the time had come for us to sort out our problems.

Great in theory. But I soon discovered in practice it was like bloody hard work. I wanted to talk about Mick and where Mum intended taking that relationship. Mum told me that was between her and the ginger nut.Then there was the problem of granddad. She'd promised to keep him off my back.

For the past week, he'd been complaining of chest pains. A visit to the doctor proved fruitless. I prayed there was something seriously wrong with him. That was very cruel, but so what? Even though he was ill, he wouldn't leave me be.

The next day Sameena came round to see me. Her future mother-in-law had written to her dad. She wanted her to come to Pakistan in July. That didn't impress Sameena. She was terrified of leaving Bradford. Uncle Naveed had made too many promises and hadn't asked Sameena what she thought. I suggested she discuss it with him openly. Sameena told me that was the worst idea I'd ever come up with.

We were deep in conversation when the sound of Granddad's slippers slapping across the passage reached our ears. I told her to carry on as though we were alone. That was bound to cause a bit of a stir.

Sameena grinned, 'Stacey, it's alright for you to talk. You don't know what it's like.'

'What's going on?' Granddad poured himself a glass of juice.

'He'll listen to you, Sammy. Your dad's not so unreasonable. I know him very well.' Brushing my fringe out of my eyes, I added, 'Before I forget, I bought you a going-away present.'

Granddad had another try. 'I asked you a question, girl.'

Sameena was enjoying herself.

Granddad slurped his juice rudely on purpose.

I glared at him. He looked bloody ancient, with his white hair and hunched back. His hand shook as he raised the glass to his mouth.

'Don't you bloody ignore me. I'm talking to you.'

'We don't want to talk with you,' I said vindictively. 'It's a silver chain, Sammy. You'll like it.'

She giggled. 'Thanks, Stacey. You didn't have to.'

'I wanted to. We're mates and cousins. Families are meant to stick together.' I was killing myself. Trying to provoke Granddad was good fun. It was impossible for him to control his temper.

His eyes flashed angrily at me. 'Are you trying to tell me something girl? You're skating on thin ice.'

I ignored him. 'Sammy, I'm back with Hasan again.'

Sameena was the perfect acting partner. 'Really?' she asked in wide-eyed surprise, 'how come?'

'He said it was stupid us being apart when we were meant to be together. We want to give it another go. I'm going out with him tonight.'

'You bloody well aren't,' yelled Granddad.

'Did you hear something?' Sameena asked.

I shook my head. The urge to laugh was overwhelming.

Granddad looked like he'd been kicked in the false teeth. 'Now you look here,' he hissed, 'I don't know what kind of game you're playing, but I'm warning you it'd better stop now.'

'Go away,' I snapped, 'this is a private conversation!'

'No, it isn't. Does your mother know you're going out with that Paki?'

'As a matter of fact she does, so put that in your pipe and smoke it.'

He didn't know I was lying. He was so angry and threatened he'd have something to say when Mum got in.

Unable to resist, I replied a whoopee cushion had more to say than him. That sent Sameena off into uncontrollable fits of laughter.

Granddad clenched his fists and told her to leave. She refused. According to him, Sameena was leading me astray. What a joke! I could do that without any help from her. He was getting more and more upset and I jumped out of my skin when he threw the glass he was holding at me. It barely missed my face.

'Next time I'll make sure it hits you,' he threatened. 'One of these days, you'll go too far, girl.'

I jumped to my feet. 'You're bloody crazy, that almost hit me.'

He gave me a venomous look. 'You're a little tart!'

'Don't you swear at me! I'm going to tell Mum when she gets in.'

'Go ahead. It's your word against mine. She's too busy chasing that ginger-haired lunatic to take any notice of you.'

'Is that so?' asked Mum.

Nobody had heard her come into the house. Granddad swung round. 'Carla, come on in.'

'Don't you Carla me. I can't believe my ears! What does it take to make you happy, Dad?' She stood with her hands on her hips.

Granddad looked unperturbed. 'What are you going on about, lass?'

'Oh, don't come the innocent with me,' she returned. 'I heard everything.'

Granddad turned pale and bit his lower lip. 'I don't feel well,' he moaned.

'Liar!' I drawled.

'Stacey, leave him alone. I'm sick to death of both of you. Dad, you go on up to bed. I'll have a word with you later.'

Granddad's face lit up with malignant anger. 'Don't you order me about,' he cried. His voice had risen and it crackled with fury. 'This is all your fault. You brought her up badly. Look at her. She dresses like a boy and she acts like a whore!'

For once in my life, I was speechless! That's not the kind of thing you expect a grandparent to come out with.

Sameena stared at Granddad in shock.

Mum didn't know what to say.

The three of us watched as he stormed out of the kitchen in a huff. Mum sat down. 'Sameena, pour me a cup of coffee.'

'Mum,' I said, 'what about...'

'Leave it, Stacey. I've had a rough day.' She took the mug from Sameena and went into the living room.

When somebody says something nasty, anger makes me react in a weird sort of way. Granddad had called me a whore. I wanted to wring his wrinkly neck. Mum must have spoken to him because he kept out of my way for a few days.

On Tuesday, I'd come back from signing on. It was a wonderful warm day and I decided to soak up some sunshine. The lawn felt soft under my bare feet and the scent from the rose bush drifted in the soft breeze.

I sat back, browsed through the magazine Sameena had lent me and put on sunglasses. The warm sun on the back of my neck made me feel sleepy. A shadow appeared over the magazine. I looked up to see Granddad standing behind me. A strange sensation ran the full length of my body. Alarm bells rang in my head. I got quickly to my feet. His face was pasty-coloured and he hadn't shaved. What distressed me was the peculiar way he kept looking at me.

'What do you want?'

'To see the back of you, you little troublemaker.'

I'd never been intimidated by him before. Every time he'd confronted me, I'd managed to stand firm. That day he scared me. He was holding a belt in his hand.

'I should have taken the strap to you a long time ago,' he sneered.

'You dare touch me,' I threatened with false bravado, 'and I'll scream.'

'Go ahead, you little Paki shit! There's nobody here to hear you.' He raised the belt, then brought it down. It cut through the air and struck me on the arm. Again, he brought it down. Pain made me wild with anger. I tried to take a firm hold of the belt. He refused to let go.

'You little bitch, I've taken enough lip from you.' Pulling the belt forward, he took me with it. Then he caught hold of me and slapped my face hard. 'It's time to sort you out, girl.'

I pushed him away. He stumbled and lost his footing. I watched in horror as he fell to the ground with a loud thud. A groan escaped from his mouth.

'Get up, you old fool,' I ordered.

He didn't move. And I couldn't move. I was rooted to the ground. Voices came from inside the house, Mum's I could clearly distinguish. Had I killed him? If he died, I'd get sent to prison and Mum would never forgive me for murdering her dad.

She called out, 'Stacey, there's somebody here I'd like you to meet.'

My mouth had gone dry. When I tried to swallow, the lump in my throat prevented me from doing so.

Another voice said, 'There's someone outside, Carla.'

I heard their voices and saw their faces but couldn't speak. Mum took one look at Granddad and almost fainted. Mick was more practical. He yelled at her to call an ambulance. Mum eyed me suspiciously and demanded what had happened. Mick told her to get a move on. She dashed off into the house. I watched as Mick bent down and checked Granddad's pulse. 'Go inside kid,' he said kindly. 'You look all done in.'

'He attacked me,' I pointed to the belt on the ground.

'We can talk later. Go on in.'

I went into my room and closed the door. In the distance, a siren sounded. Stretching out on my bed, I closed my eyes and wished, wished, I didn't know what I wished.

After what seemed like an age, Mum and Mick came back from the hospital. Granddad was going to be fine.

Mick had an amiable face. He was trying to break the ice. Mum looked tired. Her eyes were red-rimmed and swollen. I told her what had happened.

All she said was, 'You and him are both as bad as each other. When he gets out of hospital I want you to keep out of his way.'

I'd been expecting a long lecture. Luckily, I escaped with a warning. It served Granddad right. He'd been asking for trouble and he'd got it.

Mick introduced himself.

I couldn't get used to Mum going out with another man, and asked her to let me call her boyfriend by his name.

Mick said I could and shook my hand firmly. Maybe with time we could be friends.

Granddad came home from hospital the next day. Mum went up to his room with him. I was told to keep out of the way.

There was nothing to do at home so I took myself off to Sameena's. She had two days left before she departed for Pakistan. In a way, I felt she was deserting me going off to Pakistan to get married! For the love of God, aren't there enough guys in Bradford?

We nattered about the wedding. Sameena wanted me there with her - not a very bright idea. She was edgy and impatient, last minute nerves. I helped her with the packing.

Staring at her suitcases which were ready to burst at the seams I said, 'Hey Sammy come and sit down for a minute.'

Tossing her hair impatiently over her shoulders, she perched herself on the end of the bed. 'What's up now?'

Sammy's pretty, a lot like her mum really, her eyes are like black bottomless pools. Her nose is small and stubby and she has a full generous mouth like Julia Roberts. But then, she's all mouth! 'Have you spoken to your dad yet? Did you tell him that you don't want to go?'

She scowled. 'I can't. It's too late!'

'Don't be daft, there's still heaps of time.'

'Yeah, sure. What do I say? Hey Dad, by the way, I've decided I'm not going to Pakistan so there. Wake up Stacey, he'll kill me!'

'You're so stupid!' I bit out, 'He can't eat you.'

Sammy shook her head and said, 'You don't know him like I do. Dad made a promise to his sister he has every intention of keeping. I wish I didn't have to go!'

I felt sorry for her. What was Uncle Naveed thinking? It was wrong to send Sammy to a country she'd never seen before and expect her to live there. 'Tell him, Sammy. You don't have to go.' She was so stubborn at times I wanted to hit her.

'I can't!' she wailed. 'He'll never listen to me. Stacey, I'm scared.'

I admired her honesty. I'd never have admitted to any kind of fear. 'Shall I have a word with your dad?' I tried the good Samaritan cap on for size.

'You keep your big hooter out of this,' she flared up, 'this has got nothing to do with you!'

'Hang on to your wig!' I snapped. 'You're making it my business by telling me. I thought...'

'Well, don't think,' she said cutting off my sentence. 'Your thinking always gets somebody into trouble. And right now that's the last thing I bloody need.'

She paced the room like a caged animal, desperate for a taste of freedom. 'You're a coward,' I informed her. No sooner were the words out than I realised I'd put my foot in it.

Turning to me she spoke. 'Don't you call me a coward. It's alright for you to sit and talk. I'd like to see you put your money where your big gob is!' Her eyes smouldered like fiery black coals. 'This is how it's got to be.'

'Aw, come on Sammy, who are you trying to convince, me or yourself? Tell your dad, he's not a mind-reader.'

She shook her head. 'He'd never forgive me. He wants me to marry his nephew and I've got no choice.'

There was no point in continuing the discussion, Sammy had prepared herself for the worst and I could talk until I was blue in the face, it wouldn't make any difference. I left her house feeling as though all her problems were my fault. She'd be gone by the weekend and I'd have nobody to keep me company.

Saturday morning arrived too soon. I got out of bed slowly and took a shower. I'd promised to go with Sammy and her dad to the airport. My heart felt heavy. I was dreading what was to come. After a light breakfast of toast and coffee I left the house and made my way to Sammy's. It was going to be a nice day, it was mild and the sky was a vivid blue. Uncle Naveed's delivery van was parked outside the house. Arif was busy putting suitcases in the back.

'Where's Sammy?' I asked, approaching him.

'In the living room checking her stuff,' he said grumpily.

'What's up with you?'

'Dad! He made me get up at five just to be on the safe side.'

I laughed at him and walked up the path. Sameena greeted me with a watery smile. She looked tense, her hair was tied back in a pony-tail and she wore a white salvaar kameez. 'You okay?'

'I'll live,' she said heaving a sigh. 'Thanks for coming, Stacey.'

'I couldn't let you go all that way on your own.'

Uncle Naveed came out of the bathroom.'Are you ready, Sameena?'

She nodded. I noticed how her mouth trembled. Aunt Razia followed us out of the house and stood by the van.

Sammy put her arms around her mum and hugged her. Uncle Naveed wanted to leave, he was so impatient! Aunt Razia was crying. My sympathies were with her - she was against the marriage. It must have been awful for her to watch her only daughter getting ready to travel all that way and not know when they'd meet again. Watching them hugging and crying was too much for me. I got into the van and sat down on the back seat.

The drive to Manchester didn't take long. Sameena maintained a kind of silence that made me feel nervous. She sat stiffly and stared out of the window. I knew she wasn't admiring the scenery. A muscle in the side of her jaw twitched continuously.

When all the luggage was checked in Sameena said her farewells. Her dad gave her a roll of money and said, 'Behave yourself and don't let me down.'

Arif hugged her and whispered something in her ear. Then, all of a sudden, it was my turn. 'Have a safe journey,' I said weakly, not really knowing what to say. 'Write to me.'

Sammy took me by surprise. As she hugged me, she said, 'Don't let him run your life, Stacey. If you do you'll regret it.' Then turning on her heel, she walked away.

On the way back to Bradford, I decided the time had come for me to try and make a new life for myself as far away as possible from Mum and the rest of my grotty family. The prospect of having my own place and doing exactly what I liked was very appealing. The more thought I gave it, the more the idea lodged itself in my mind. I knew Mum wouldn't have any objections. At least I wouldn't have to put up with Granddad any more. As I went into our house, I found myself thinking about Sammy. She'd be preparing herself for a life away from everything she was used to. I still felt sorry for her! Deciding not to launch straight into battle with Mum until the time was right I hung around doing nothing much for the rest of the day.

The next morning I didn't get the chance to tell Mum what I'd decided. Granddad was complaining of chest pains and Mum didn't want to leave him. At first, I thought that the old fool was faking it, but one look at his grey face told me there was something wrong with him. Mum took a tray up and returned with it a few minutes later. 'He won't eat,' she informed me. 'I'm worried, Stacey. I'd better call the doctor.'

While Mum was on the 'phone, Mick turned up. 'Hi,' he said, 'is your mum in?'

'She's on the 'phone,' I replied as I closed the door behind him.

'What's up?'

Pulling a face, I told him that Granddad was feeling off colour. Mick offered to drive him straight up to the hospital. Mum had her work cut out for her helping Granddad dress. He did nothing but moan and groan. Every now and then, his face would turn ashen.

'Shall I help you?' I asked Mum as she bent down and helped Granddad put his shoes on.

'She can manage,' he wheezed. 'Leave us alone. '

'Dad, don't be like that,' Mum scolded. 'She's only trying to help.'

Lying back on the bed, he said, 'Should have got rid of her when you had the chance, Carla.'

'Aw shut your face,' I spat out and ran out of the room.

From a distance, I watched Mum and Mick guide Granddad to the car.

My mind flashed back to the time when Dad had died and Mum had to go to the hospital. I felt my stomach muscles tighten, I pressed my hand against the door and stood motionless. The engine roared into life and the car moved off. I waited for Mum to call from hospital. God alone knows why. After all, I hated his bloody guts. Bored out of my head, I went up to my room and switched on the telly.

It was dark when the car pulled up outside. I turned the volume down and hurried out of my room. Mick was leading Mum into the house. She looked all washed-out. Her eyes were swollen and the tip of her nose was red.

'Mum, what's up?'

Her lower lip trembled. 'Dad's dead!' She broke into a sob.

I couldn't believe my ears. 'What!'

'Heart attack,' said Mick. 'Go and make your mum a cuppa.'

In a state of euphoric shock I allowed my feet to carry me to the kitchen. Wow! Granddad was dead! It was too good to be true.

I plugged in the kettle and tried to contain my joy. With Granddad out of the way, I was free. 'How are you?' asked Mick, startling me. I hadn't heard him come in. I wheeled round to face him. 'I'm fine. Tell me what happened.'

'Heart attack on the way to the hospital. The doctor tried to revive him but he was too late. Don't take it too hard. He was old.'

Mick made me want to laugh.

'Do me a favour, Stacey. Your mum's upset. Keep an eye on her for me.'

'Sure thing.' I handed him his mug and went to comfort Mum.

Three glorious days after, Uncle Naveed appeared to take us to Nab Wood Cemetery. Granddad had wanted to be cremated. I didn't want to attend the service and knew I'd feel like a hypocrite standing by the grave, dressed in black trying to look as sober as death itself. But I dragged myself along for Mum's sake. She was crying into her hankie.

There weren't many people; that didn't surprise me, Granddad hadn't been very popular. The vicar said the famous words, 'Ashes to ashes, dust to dust.' I couldn't wipe the grin off my face as I added under my breath, 'If the Lord don't take you then the devil must.'

With each handful of soil that hit the coffin, I knew the old git was gone for good.

It took a while for things to get back to normal and that meant that I couldn't approach Mum with my intentions. She was naturally upset and I knew it'd take her ages to forget about her dad, even though he'd been a tyrant!

At least with Granddad gone I could relax. He couldn't boss me about and tell me what to do. That guy had really known how to bear a grudge. Never once in all his life had he accepted me as his granddaughter. Not that I cared anymore, he was dead and I still had my life in front of me.

Mum went back to work and I took it as a sign she was fit to cope with my news.

She was slightly pale and looked tired, but otherwise she seemed to be alright.

Mick was coming around a lot more, I don't think Granddad had approved of him either. That night as Mum sat nursing her cup of hot chocolate, I made up my mind to break it to her. Unfortunately I didn't get the chance. Just when I was getting ready, she informed me she was going up to bed. Sighing heavily, I let her go, she had given me some more time to plan what I'd say to her. I thought it would be easy to make her see reason, but Mum proved to be no pushover!

The next day after breakfast I told Mum about my big decision. She really knocked me for six when she didn't agree with me. I thought that she'd be the last person to try and put a spanner in the works. But then parents are very unpredictable creatures, aren't they? They always think they know what's best for you, even though it's not what you want. Mum shook her head and said, 'No Stacey, I want you here with me.'

'But why?'

'There's no real reason why. You can't support yourself financially and it's not a good idea. '

'Mum, I do get dole!'

'Stacey, wake up. You can't live on what you're getting. Who's going to pay the bills and buy the things that you need?'

'I'll manage somehow.'

'No, you won't because you're not going anywhere!'

Mum seemed pretty certain she could bully me into doing exactly what she wanted. I had to stand on my own two feet. 'Mum, I'm not going to the moon. I just want to move out. That's not such a big thing.'

'Yes it is! I want you to live with me.'

'Come on, Mum. Are you worried about being on your own? You've got Mick now and Uncle Naveed and his lot live just down the road.'

'At least they all know the meaning of the word loyalty,' she said spitefully.

'What the hell is that meant to mean?' I was angry. When Mum was upset or annoyed, she'd start to clean up. I could tell she was about to have one of her turns. She brought out the fluffy pink duster. 'You're so selfish, Stacey,' she informed me as the pink monster in her hands whipped the curtains, 'you offer a person a little bit of friendship and when it's about to be tested, you withdraw it completely.'

She picked up a cushion, fluffed it out and placed it on the coffee table, while she dusted the armchair with a vigour she'd not displayed for a long time. 'Have you ever loved anybody in your life?'

That was an awful thing to ask me. I couldn't respond. She moved over to the fireplace and rearranged the awful figurines she'd collected over the years. For the first time in my life, I had nothing to say. Mum took this as an invitation to really lay the boot in. 'Take a long hard look at yourself, Stacey. All you ever do is scowl.Why do you treat people like dirt? All my life I've had to look after other people,' she paused for a breath and glared at me. 'You always want your own way and when you can't have it you sulk. Well, this time, girl, you're going to do as I say.'

Picking a magazine up off the floor, I rolled it up tightly and held on to it. What I really wanted to do was hit Mum with it. That would have shown her how I was feeling.

'Are you going to sit there like a cabbage?' she asked cruelly.

'No I'm not!' I defended myself. 'I love you and the rest of my family and you've got no right to talk me like that.'

She scoffed. 'Don't make me laugh. You love your family? That's the biggest joke I've ever heard.'

'Well that's too bad,' I spat out, 'I'm going to do what I like.'

Mum wagged a finger in my face. 'Treat people the way you expect to be treated.'

'What are you going on about?' I was baffled by her outburst.

'Arif,' she said dramatically. 'You treat him like dirt.'

'That's because he is dirt.' I shot back. I didn't mean to say it, but Mum wanted a fight. 'I can't stand the sight of him, the useless shit!'

Her hand connected with my face in a sharp, stinging slap. 'Mark my words, girl, that big mouth of yours is going to get you into a lot of trouble one day. You make fun of everybody and think you're better than the rest of us.'

Talk about blowing things out of proportion. All I wanted was to leave home. Mum was set on starting the third world war. She continued to vent her anger. 'Whenever I've needed you, Stacey, you've never been here. I wanted you to be happy and all you've ever done is go around with your lower lip touching the ground. Mick and the rest of the family aren't going to make up for a daughter. But then, what sort of a daughter leaves her mother at the drop of a hat?'

She was feeling sorry for herself and wanted my sympathy. 'Mum, you're the one who's always put other people before me. You couldn't decide whether your dad was more important than your daughter.' I cringed knowing perfectly I'd jumped in feet first. I'd wanted to say she'd considered her dad as top priority and I didn't figure in any of her plans.

Mum must have known what I was going on about. She had to make excuses for the man even when he was dead! 'Your Granddad's bark was worse than his bite. He loved you.'

I laughed hysterically. 'What a load of bull! He didn't know the meaning of the word.' I went and switched on the TV.

'Then that makes two of you,' she snapped and flicked it off. 'Don't provoke me, Stacey.'

Catching me off guard, she seized my arm and shoved me down onto the couch. 'You move from there and I won't be responsible for my actions.'

'You tried to get rid of me,' I screamed at her, 'and don't you try to deny it.'

'For your information, young lady, I didn't get rid of you. Your father was the most important person in my life and when he died I found I couldn't cope. The family you hate so much helped me to get back on my feet. They looked after you for me.'

Sitting down, she buried her face in her hands. I couldn't tell whether or not she was crying. The urge to comfort her was there, but I was scared of her rejecting me. Looking at me, she continued. 'Dad hassled me all the time, that's why you had to go to your Uncle Naveed's. His nagging was driving me up the wall.'

I felt a sudden surge of self-pity. 'You weren't there when I needed you. There was nobody who could understand the sort of torment I was going through.'

'Don't you try and swing this your way!' she snapped vehemently. 'What the hell do you think it was like for me when you walked out of here behaving like a snooty little madam. Dad did nothing but gloat. I was so ashamed of you for letting me down.'

I opened my mouth to speak. 'Don't,' she said holding up her hand, 'I'm sick of you.'

'Yeah, well, the feeling's mutual,' I grumbled.

Mum glared at me. 'Get out!' she yelled, 'Get out of my sight, I'm sick to death of you.'

'Where shall I go?'

'Where shall I go,' she mimicked sarcastically, 'You're the one who wanted to move out, so leave. And this time don't bother coming back.'

Standing rather reluctantly, I said, 'I'll go to Uncle Naveed. At least he won't turn me away.'

'Oh get lost, Stacey! You expect me to fall for that old trick again. Pack your stuff and get out of my house. From now on, I wash my hands of you.' Her hair bounced up and down as she walked out in a rage. My mouth hung open like a stunned fish.

Mum had told me to leave and that was exactly what I was going to do. Up in my room I pulled out my rucksack from under the bed and stuffed my clothes into it. Lifting the mattress I took out my purse and put it in my pocket.

Leaving the house, I walked like a person without a care in the world. The fair had come to town. The whole place was a buzz of sounds and people. The music, beating like a heart in the middle of the park, caught my attention. A kaleidoscope of colourful caravans and stalls littered the grounds. So engrossed was I in my own world that I didn't see Arif skulking in the bushes. Jumping out from his hiding place, he said, 'Well, well, well, if it isn't Stacey.'

He scared me out of my skin. 'What the hell! You almost gave me a heart attack.'

54

He grinned broadly and fell into step with me, the fact that I hadn't invited him to join me didn't put him off.

'What, no bad language? You disappoint me, cousin dear. Here I was looking forward to washing out your gob with soap, what a letdown you are.'

Laughter rumbled in his throat. I wasn't in the mood for his brand of humour. 'Why is it you're always lurking about like a bad smell?'

'Just keeping an eye on you,' he said cheekily. 'It's not safe for you to be out on your own.'

'Are you pulling my leg?'

'Do you want me to?'

'Don't be daft!' I snapped and sat down under Lister's monument.

'What's with the rucksack?' he eyed it with undisguised disgust. 'It could do with a wash.'

'I'm going away for a while.'

'Where to?' The music almost drowned his voice and filled the summer air.

'None of your business.' I brushed a tendril of hair from my face.

'Come on, Stacey, what gives?'

'What's it to you?'

'Don't like secrets,' he replied in a sulky voice. 'Come on, Stacey, where are you off to?'

'Buy me a candy and I'll tell you.'

'Okay, you wait here and I'll be back.' He sauntered off towards the candy stall.

I swung the rucksack onto my back, ran out of the park and came to an abrupt halt at the roadside. Damn! The traffic tailed for miles. Winding my way through the cars, I ran until the sweat poured down my face. It was getting warm and the rucksack banged against my back every time I moved.

'Hey Stacey,' yelled the familiar voice I'd been trying to get away from. Arif was in hot pursuit, I stopped in my tracks and watched him. He was red and scowling, with pink candy floss wobbling in his hand. Bits of it were flying away in his haste to catch me up. He looked so comical, I couldn't help laughing. 'You rotten cow, that was a nasty thing to do.'

Putting my arms around his neck I laughed some more. He pushed me away. 'Get off me, you're mad. I swear you are. Here's your candy floss. What a waste of money that was.' He held out the stick with a tuft of fluff left on it. 'What kind of game are you playing?' he demanded.

'Can't you take a joke?'

'That wasn't funny Stacey! Now spit it out, where are you going?' It was obvious he wasn't going to give up. 'Mum chucked me out.'

'Wow, no kidding!'

The thought of me being homeless apparently thrilled him.

'So now you know. I'd better be on my way. See you around Arif.'

'Hang on a sec, I'll go with you. Where are you heading?'

'Come off it Arif!' I complained, 'I'm going on my own. What the hell do you want to tag along for?' The guy was really out of his tree.

Shrugging his shoulders, he smiled at me. 'Things aren't really going my way at home. Dad wants me to marry you. He can't get it into his thick head I'm not prepared to do that.'

We walked slowly towards town. Raising my eyebrows in amazement, I said, 'I can't believe how bloody arrogant you are. There's no way I'd marry you. So don't let's go into all that again.'

'Hang onto your wig woman,' he snapped, 'and pass me that filthy rucksack.' He held out his hand. I was glad to be rid of the blasted thing. 'For your information Stacey, this marriage business wasn't my idea. You know what my dad's like when he wants his own way. He doesn't give a damn about anybody else.' He heaved the rucksack onto his back. 'He's the one who wants an idiot like you for a daughter-in-law. So, come on, what happened with your mum?'

'I told her I wanted to leave home. I can't understand why she got so heavy about it. I tell you, Arif, we don't speak the same language any more! Mum said that I'm selfish!'

'Can't think why,' he said.

'Whose side are you on?'

'I'm not taking sides,' he informed me majestically.

'What am I going to do?' I asked him. We walked towards the city centre. Arif grinned at me.

'It's not that bad. You wanted to move out and your mum gave you the go ahead.'

'You don't understand! I didn't want to part on hostile terms with her.

That only means that I can't go back when the going gets rough. Mum's a right cow!'

'She's had enough hassles, Stacey,' Arif said seriously. 'Give her a break!'

I fell silent and thought about what he said. Granddad and Arif had made enough trouble for me. I knew if I opened my mouth to speak, Arif and I would end up fighting so I fumed inwardly. My life had been nothing but a disaster so far and it didn't look like it was getting any better. Maybe Mum chucking me out was a good thing. At least I'd be able to blame her if I didn't manage to make a go of things on my own.

'Arif, I'd better get a shuffle on or the ticket station will close.'

He caught hold of my arm. 'Stacey, Dad wants me to take care of you. He reckons it's my duty to see that nothing happens to you.'

I felt my hackles rise. 'I'm quite capable of doing that without your help. Tell you dad to butt out of my life!'

'It's time we buried the hatchet,' he informed me.

'I'd love to - right in the back of your head!'

Arif wagged a finger at me. 'If me wasn't such a gentleman, me'd be tempted to wring your scrawny little neck.'

'Try it mate,' I tempted him.

Arif wouldn't let me go to the station. Instead he offered me a place in his house claiming that Uncle Naveed wouldn't mind. I knew they'd have no objections to my living with them again. But the thought of seeing Mum wasn't very appealing. After a lot of pushing and coaxing, he managed to talk me round. As we turned and headed for his house I found myself thinking what a failure I was. I couldn't even leave home by myself. Arif had insisted that a damsel in distress needed helping, I didn't fit the bill.

As we neared the house, Arif tugged my sleeve. 'If Dad tries to bully you, let me handle him.'

I got quite a shock when we pushed open the gate and stepped into the paved yard. Uncle Naveed stood in the doorway looking as forbidding as the angel of death. Arif and I exchanged puzzled glances.

'Where have you been?'

I stammered, 'Erm....I....well....I....' My bloody lips were behaving like they'd been stitched up.

Arif intervened. 'She was with me Dad.'

'Inside now,' he bellowed like a mad bull, 'come on, move.'

Arif muttered under his breath, 'What's up with him?'

I decided not to reply. The sight of Mum sitting on the couch really threw me. Not another showdown. I couldn't take much more.

'Sit down, both of you,' shouted Uncle Naveed. He was pretty worked up about something and I was willing to bet that Mum had a hand in whatever it was that had upset him. Arif dragged himself to the couch, he sat slowly. A shot of laughter burst from my mouth.

'What is funny?' asked Uncle Naveed. 'You have got some explaining to do, young lady.'

'I've not done anything.' The living room seemed awfully hot, despite the fact that the windows were wide open. The white net curtain billowed like a cloud blown about in the sky. The sound of children drifted into the room. I wished I was a kid again, out of trouble and innocent to the realities of life.

'Are you listening to me Stacey?' asked Uncle Naveed.

I looked up in a daze. 'What did you say?'

'Wake up girl,' he scolded. 'Why are you always out to make trouble for everybody?' He was on the warpath and I was to be his victim. I stared at my shoes, they were crying out for a good polishing.

Uncle Naveed continued his lecture. 'I went over to your house hoping to find that simpleton over there,' he pointed a finger at Arif. I struggled with the snigger, God, the effort was killing me! A small titter rose from the pit of my stomach. 'I found your mother in a distressing state. You, as usual, were nowhere in sight. What are you up to?'

'Mum chucked me out!'

Mum gave me a filthy look and said, 'You wanted to move out so don't blame me!'

Wow, I told myself. She has a tongue after all. Pity she doesn't use the thing more often in my defence.

Aunt Razia got to her feet. 'I am going to make a pot of tea.' I watched her leave us to sort out the trouble which had been brewing for so long.

Uncle Naveed didn't sit down. He towered over me like the Grim Reaper. 'You cannot move out. Your mother needs you at home.'

He must have taken my silence as a very big yes, because he said,

'When your mother goes home, you will be going with her. I have always had high hopes for you, do not let me down.'

Moving across the floor quietly, he turned his attention to Arif who was busy chewing a matchstick. It dangled out of his mouth, he rolled it across his bottom lip over and over again.

'Take that blasted thing out of your mouth.'

Arif reluctantly removed the offending object and put it into his pocket. The poor guy had to sit and listen to his dad showering abuse down on his head. Didn't he know he was a disgrace to the family? Arif merely shrugged and looked quite resigned.

It was amusing to observe his reactions. For one who always acted so cool he looked slightly hot under the collar. Things didn't seem so enjoyable any more. Then Uncle Naveed said, 'You think you can deceive me Arif. Well, you are very much mistaken. I know about your lady friend.'

Arif looked him straight in the eye and said, 'So what if you do? There's not much that you can do about it.'

Uncle Naveed sneered at him. 'Do not provoke me, Arif! That is the worst thing you could do at the moment.'

'Look, Dad. What I do with my life has got nothing to do with you at all!'

I cringed as Uncle Naveed shot Arif a look of pure contempt. The guy was out of his mind, pushing his dad like that. 'You are wrong, Arif. What you do is my business. I am not going to let you flaunt yourself in public with an Indian girl.' There was anger in his eyes and he was trying very hard to control his fury.

'I'm old enough to know my own mind!' Arif flashed back.

'Do not talk to me about what you think you know. I am your father. In this house, there is only one Malik and you are looking at him.' Uncle Naveed shook a fist in Arif's face. He, in turn, flinched away. 'If you are so grown up, please be so good as to tell me why I am still supporting you?'

'How come you're so annoyed?'

That was not a very wise question to ask considering the dark scowl and reply he received. 'You seem to think a good job will be handed to you on a silver plate.'

Arif interrupted him, 'I work for you, Dad, so you can't say I don't!'

'That is not work,' thundered Uncle Naveed. 'Wake up, boy, this is the real world. Driving to Birmingham and Dewsbury once in a while does not mean anything to me. Get up off your backside and show me what you are made off.'

Standing up, Arif shot him a poisonous look. He was like a bull about to charge. 'I'm going to do what I like and you're not going to stop me!'

'Not in my house!' yelled Uncle Naveed. 'There is no way you are going to make me into the laughing stock of Bradford. Everywhere I go people will say, take a look at that old fool, his son has an Indian girlfriend. I will not stand by and let that happen.' He slammed his fist against the wall. The violent look in his eyes was terrifying. All Arif had to do was say one word out of place and Uncle Naveed would explode.

Arif gave his dad a defiant glare and said, 'Who gives a shit what people say? I'm old enough to make my own decisions. I'm not Sameena and you can't boss me about. You were desperate to get Sameena married off to the first loser that came along. You ruled her life and ruined everything for her. There's no way I'm going to let you do that to me!'

Uncle Naveed turned ashen. 'Stacey, do you think I bullied my daughter into marriage?'

Mum interrupted. 'Come on, Naveed, what does she know? You won't ever get an honest answer out of her.'

'No Carla, she was her best friend. Tell me Stacey, did I force Sameena?' The fat was most certainly in the fire now.

'She seemed happy enough to me,' I replied knowing very well that I was telling an awful lie. I faced a situation where the Uncle I loved and respected was asking me for an honest opinion. There was no way I could hurt his feelings. The easy solution was to massage the truth.

'Sammy was fine,' I repeated. 'You never forced her into anything. He doesn't know what he's talking about.' Talk about the rat deserting the sinking ship! I was no better.

Uncle Naveed seemed satisfied with my reply and turned to Arif. 'I know that I cannot force you to marry Stacey. However, I have taken steps to make sure that you do not see your girlfriend again. I am not going to sit back and let you drag somebody else down with you.'

'What can you bloody do about it. You can't stop me from seeing Kashmir!'

'I already have.'

'What?'

'I went to see your lady friend and her family this morning. You are lucky they did not carve you up. They were itching to get their hands on you. If you hurry, Arif, you will be able to wave Kashmir off from Manchester Airport.'

My mouth fell open in horror. Uncle Naveed wasn't so cruel! Arif looked like he'd been struck by lightning. His handsome face had turned a sickly yellow colour.

Arif went mad. He was screaming and shouting like crazy. I really felt sorry for him. Uncle Naveed and Mum sat back and watched tongue-tied, while Arif flipped his lid! It was alright for them to drive the guy to the brink of insanity. For the first time in my life I watched silently as Arif sat down and cried. That wasn't a pleasant sight. I'd totally dismissed the people around me as being petrified where feelings were concerned. To see Arif displaying his emotions so openly was a right shock to the system.

I wanted to comfort him, he looked really fed-up. Slowly, Arif got to his feet and walked towards the door. 'Where are you going?' I called after him.

He offered no reply, the slamming door told me all I needed to know. Uncle Naveed made sure I went home with Mum. He took us in his car, that way I couldn't refuse.

That night curled up in bed, I ran over the day's happenings. There didn't appear to be any sequence, just a jumble of muddled thoughts tripping over each other in fast forward. Where was Arif? I couldn't help worrying about him. Did he have a bed for the night? No matter how I tossed and turned, sleep wouldn't come. He had my sympathy wherever he was.

A week elapsed and nobody had seen anything of Arif. Uncle Naveed was slightly concerned, I could tell from his face. He was so used to concealing his feelings that talking to him about Arif was quite difficult. Aunt Razia, on the other hand, was always ready with a chat and a cup of tea. The strain of not knowing where her son was, was obviously getting to her. I found myself reminding her constantly that Arif wasn't a kid and he could take care of himself. This didn't help to calm her down. She confided in me that she and Uncle Naveed were fighting because of the kids and she wanted to get away for a while.

Aunt Razia was very secretive when it came down to her relationship with her husband. She always kept quiet no matter what was bothering her. The trouble between Uncle Naveed and Arif had taken its toll. She sat down and cried. She cried for Sammy who was thousands of miles away from home, a girl needed her mother on her wedding day. Yet Uncle Naveed had deprived his wife of that joy by shipping Sammy off to Pakistan on her own. I was of no help to Aunt Razia. I did feel sorry for her and cursed Arif and Uncle Naveed for causing her so much pain. Arif needed a good hard kick in the pants for upsetting his mother.

At home, relations between Mum and me were slightly strained. She only spoke when it was necessary, and even then I got the feeling that she didn't really want to. She had started staying out until all hours with Mick, and when they did get in, they made enough noise to wake the flaming dead! I wanted to get away as soon as possible and set about finding myself a job. Half-heartedly, I applied for a job in Leeds as a secretary and forgot all about it until a letter came summoning me for an interview, which was to take place on the tenth day of August at two thirty in the afternoon. I had one day to get myself ready for another knock back.

Up in my bedroom I rummaged around in my wardrobe for something decent to wear. Personally, jeans were a strong favourite, but I couldn't turn up for an interview in them. I needed something else. Finally, after trying all of my skirts and blouses, I settled for a pastel pink frock that mum had bought me for my birthday. It was perfect. All I needed was a jacket. Mum had been out buying herself a new image, it would be alright to borrow from her just as long as she didn't find out.

Sneaking into her room while she was downstairs watching telly, I went through her wardrobe and found a long, white cardigan with pearl buttons. I was sure she wouldn't miss it and anyway my need was greater than hers. Pulling it off the plastic hanger, I took it into my room and hid it under my mattress.

Mick had changed Mum into a different person. She went out three nights a week with him and it looked like she was having more fun than me. How come I couldn't find someone to hang out with and my geriatric mother could? Sometimes life was so cruel!

The next day, I woke with a lead balloon weighing down my stomach. I was too jumpy to eat. After a quick shower, I cleaned my bedroom and sat down in front of the mirror and pulled faces to pass the time. Mum was at work and the house was very quiet.

I watched telly for a while and then decided to get ready. Dressing carefully so I wouldn't crease my dress, I put on the slightest bit of make-up. My hair needed cutting, but for now it would have to do. Taking a handful from each side of my head, I secured it in the middle with a hair clip. Mum's cardigan really suited me, it had shoulder pads and for a second I felt like an actress from 'Dynasty'.

I checked my purse for change, went downstairs and gulped down a glass of apple juice. On the bus journey, I planned all the things I was going to say. My hands felt really clammy.

I found the rather majestic looking Rhodes and Co on the quiet side of town. I pushed open the huge glass doors and went inside to the carpetted foyer. A young woman sat at the reception desk looking as bored as hell. She gave me directions in her nasal whine and informed me that the lift wasn't working. Bloody typical! By the time I got to the fifth floor, with my fitness record, I wouldn't be able to stand, let alone open my mouth.

The interview took all of five minutes. I sat in a stuffy little office with a woman called Mrs Carpenter. She really got on my nerves. Every time she asked me a question she would sit back and stare at her nails. I got the feeling they were of more importance than hiring a new secretary. And she asked bloody stupid questions which I answered as politely as I could even though I was thinking terrible thoughts.

'Well, Miss Malik, please tell me why you want this job.'

I could have said I was sick of signing on, my mum was in an old folks' home and I needed the money to pay her medical bills.

Instead, I smiled tartly at her and replied. 'It's just what I trained for. The job sounds exciting and I feel ready for a challenge.' How corny! Typing letters wasn't challenging.

Then she went on and asked me whether or not I had any work experience. I wanted to say that walking up all those steps was enough work experience to last me a lifetime. But of course I didn't. I told her the truth and that was like giving the hangman a bit more rope to make a noose. She listened, nodding occasionally, and then dismissed me. I went home feeling rather deflated.

Two days later a letter arrived informing me I'd been given the job. I felt sorry for the idiots. They were in for a shock!

I congratulated myself and went to find Mum, who was making her bed. 'Mum, I've got something to tell you.' I sat down on the ottoman.

'What's up?' she fluffed out a frothy, pink-laced pillow.

'I've got a job!'

'Really?' She stared at me in disbelief. I bet she'd been thinking I was bloody useless and would be forever on the scrounge!

'Job starts in September. I'm really looking forward to it.'

'I'm really pleased for you. It's about time you had something to do.'

Grinning, I said. 'I can't wait, Mum. This is just what I need. I'm off out to see Aunt Razia, do you want anything?'

'Mind what you say to her. She's upset about this business with Arif and his dad.'

'I'll be careful,' I promised. 'See you later.'

The air was alive with a cocktail of sounds. A skipping rope tapped monotonously, and a girl with jet black hair jumped up and down. A gang of lads kicked a football about in the road. They shouted and cheered noisily. The drone of a lawnmower could be heard. It felt good to be alive!

Aunt Razia sat in the garden hard at work with her knitting. 'Hi,' I called as I shoved open the gate. 'What are you making?'

She looked up and gave me a smile. 'Hello, Stacey,' her voice was sad. 'Come and sit with me. I am making this for Arif.'

Squeezing her shoulder gently I flopped down on the garden seat next to her.

'How are you?'

'I am tired, Stacey, Sameena wrote a letter, she wants to come home.'

'When did it arrive?'

'This morning, your uncle says she is no longer our responsibility. She has to learn to live in Pakistan. I want her to come back home. Your grandmother is very ill, she wants to see you and Arif before....'

She didn't finish the sentence. I knew what she meant.

'I can't go to Pakistan!'

Aunt Razia shook her head slowly and put down her knitting. 'You are her eldest son's only child, Stacey.'

I chewed my lower lip. 'So what do you think?'

'I cannot think any more,' she replied, 'Arif is so angry with his father, he will never agree to such a thing.'

'Why not?'

'Because he has no intention of making his father happy. Arif came to see me yesterday. He looked awful. He has got it into his head that he has to go and find Kashmir, he asked me for money.'

I spluttered angrily. 'You're joking!'

'It is no joke, Stacey. I am his mother and if he cannot turn to me, then where will he go? Two children and both have gone. It makes me happy to see that you have not forgotten me.'

I hugged her. 'You're my mate. I can't stand it when you're unhappy. Is there anything I can do to help?'

'Go to Pakistan and bring Sameena back for me!' She replied.

'I would if I could, but I haven't got that sort of money. And besides I can't go on my own.'

'Arif would go with you. Will you ask him Stacey?'

'He'd never do it!' I exclaimed. 'Where's he living anyway?'

'On Marlborough Road, in a flat.'

'Give me the number. I'll go and see him for you.'

Aunt Razia beamed at me. 'Do not tell him that I sent you and please do not let your uncle know I talked this over with you. He will be angry.'

Promising to be discreet, I went on my mission of mercy. Aunt Razia had always been so good to me. There'd never been a day when she'd turned her back on me. Talking to Arif on her behalf was the least I could do. If she wanted me to go to Pakistan, then I would. But why was Uncle Naveed being so ruthless? There was a side to his character I'd only begun to notice and what I saw I didn't like!

Pausing on the doorstep of the huge house where Arif was living, I rang the bell to Flat Three.

'What do you want?' Arif leered down at me from the window above.

Not a very friendly reception. 'How about moving your butt and letting me in?'

His head disappeared. Footsteps sounded on the stairs. The door opened. 'Is there something I can do for you?'

'Look, Arif, I didn't come all this way to converse with you in the street. Let's go up to your room.'

Reluctantly, he stepped back and allowed me to enter. Talk about being a gentleman. He had the manners of a pig! The dark passage reeked of urine and stale tobacco smoke burnt my nostrils.

'What a stink! Who died?'

Arif didn't reply. He walked in a determined manner. A large box of newspaper stood on the second floor landing. 'You've got enough linen.' I informed him as I kicked the box and got covered by a cloud of dust.

The flat was in the attic, a kitchen, living room and bedroom all rolled into one.

'I'll tell you something,' I said sarcastically as I eyed the filthy hovel, 'you sure as hell did land on your feet, this place is neat.'

'Quit the smart talk,' he bit out. 'You know where the door is.'

'I came to tell you that I've got a job in Leeds.'

'Big deal!' he was in a foul mood. 'Do you think I'm thick? What do you really want?'

He stared at me suspiciously. His hair was a tangled mess and he needed a shave. He was shutting me out and I didn't like it. 'To see how you are,' I answered.

'As you can see, I'm fine. Did my dad tell you to spy on me?'

Under different circumstances, I'd have done just that. However the thought'd never even crossed my mind. 'Don't be daft! What do you take me for?'

'You shouldn't ask too many questions,' he sneered. 'You might not like the answers.'

'What's with you?'

'Go away, Stacey!'

'Arif, please!'

'Shove off, you're the last person I want sniffing around. Take a walk.'

'Fine if that's the way you want it,' I snapped. 'See if I bloody care. No, don't bother getting up I know where the door is.'

Salvaging my tattered pride, I tried not to run out. Arif could go to hell for all I cared. Going to him with good intentions had been a waste of time. After the way he'd spoken to me, he could forget about being my friend. What if he'd had the rug pulled out from under him, that wasn't my fault. But he was trying to lay the blame at my door. He'd been stabbed in the back and I guess the wounds hadn't been given enough time to heal. Arif's mood was upsetting, he'd always been so full of beans. Everything was a joke. Over a short period of time he'd turned into a bitter, angry person.

When I got home, Uncle Naveed was discussing something in the street with Mum. He was in quite a state. Bracing myself for the worst, I decided to walk past undetected. Mum must have eyes in the back of her head because she said. 'Stacey can you come here for a minute? We need to talk.'

That sounded ominous. Mum wanting to talk usually meant I was in for a good ear bashing. 'What's up?' I asked suspiciously as I leant against Uncle Naveed's car.

'Nothing's up. Come on, let's go inside.'

Uncle Naveed handed me a blue envelope. My hand shook slightly as I withdrew the sheet of lined writing paper. I stared at Uncle Naveed. 'Read it,' he urged impatiently, 'and tell me what you think.'

'Dear Mum and Dad,

I hope that you're both well. For days, I've been trying to convince myself I should attempt to make a go of living here. After a great deal of confusing thoughts and feelings I have to say I'm no nearer my goal. Dad, you must have received my other letters by now. I've been waiting ages for a reply. You don't know what this place is like. I really hate it.

If I have to stay here, I'm scared of what might happen to me. You made me marry a right pain in the neck! I've hardly seen him since I got here, he spends all his time with his friends.

Dad, your mother isn't well and she wants to see you. I've tried to explain you might not be able to make it. But she refuses to listen. She also wants to see Stacey and Arif. What can I do, Dad? In this place I'm not considered as a person. You gave me away without even taking the time to find out what kind of husband you got for me. It's alright for him

67

to beat me up and make me starve, you don't seem to care. I don't know how long I can live in such an environment. Please write to me. In this horrible place I need a scrap of comfort. Also see if you can send out two more lambs for the slaughter. I've got to go because the illiterate one is scowling at me. Give my love to Mum. Love Sameena.'

Aunt Razia had prepared me for this shock and I was grateful to her. 'So what do you think?' asked Uncle Naveed anxiously.

'Sammy sounds like she's having a rough time. I'm going out there.'

Mum and Uncle Naveed stared at me in stunned silence. 'Well, say something!' I said, coolly, relishing with grim satisfaction the fact they were shocked by my acceptance of such a strange proposal. 'It'll be good to see Sammy again.'

Mum sat down. 'You're certainly full of surprises. Here I was thinking we'd have to drag you kicking and screaming to the airport. I'll never be able to understand how your mind works.'

'I'm going for Sammy's sake, Mum, not because it'll make you two happy. Can't you tell from her letter she's bloody desperate? I'm only going out there for my cousin!'

Disappointment flashed across Uncle Naveed's face. Instead of being relieved, he was defeated. I guess he'd been ready for a bit of a fight.

'Cheer up, Uncle. At least you'll get your own way again.'

'What do you mean by that?' he demanded frostily.

'Nothing, it's always been me who's been in trouble for one reason or another and you and Aunt Razia have bailed me out. Just look upon this as a favour being returned. I'm prepared to go to Pakistan for you. But I can't say the same for Arif!'

Uncle Naveed ran his fingers roughly through his thick mass of hair. Dad had always done that too when frustration wouldn't let him vent his anger. 'Have you seen Arif?'

I nodded. 'He's so rude. I'm not going to pay him another visit. He's feeling sorry for himself and looking for somebody to carry the blame for him. I'm not that somebody!'

'Can't you talk him round Stacey?' Mum asked as she walked into the kitchen. We followed her through.

'No, not really,' I replied as I took the cold salad she handed me. 'He can do what he likes.'

68

Uncle Naveed sat down. 'He must hate me for what I did,' he played with the salt pot. 'Sometimes I wish I had not interfered.'

Mum patted his arm. 'Come on, Naveed, don't worry. Arif's not the type to bear a grudge for very long.'

Through a mouthful of coleslaw, I said, 'You could've fooled me. You should've seen him. He stinks like a skunk and looks like a hardened criminal.'

'Don't do that, Stacey,' Mum slapped my hand. 'How many times have I told you not to talk with your mouth filled to bursting? You act like a little kid sometimes!'

'As I was saying, he's not very pleased with you, Uncle. He threw me out!'

'Never mind that,' added Uncle Naveed. 'You can't go to Pakistan alone.'

'Sammy did, and I'm older than her.'

He told me that age had nothing to do with it and the fact that I couldn't speak Urdu proved it would be difficult for me to manage alone. I was left with no other choice but to try and talk Arif round. Talk about luck! Of all the travelling companions to get lumbered with, mine would have to be Arif. Travelling with an ape would have been more entertaining, Arif was the next best thing.

The next morning after a hearty breakfast consisting of tea and hot buttered toast with fried eggs, I went to see Arif again. Maybe I'm a glutton for punishment! It wasn't wise to rush out to a country I knew nothing about. The urge to tread new ground pushed me forward. What did I know about our family in Pakistan? Not a lot, that much I can tell you. I'd seen relatives now and then in snapshots. There'd never been any communication with them until now. Sameena's letter had been a real bombshell.

Arif, all swollen with conceit, greeted me with the same rudeness I'd encountered the previous day. How I longed to give him a slap. He was so damn arrogant. He wanted my sympathy, hell would freeze over before he got that. Talking to him was like banging my head against a brick wall. And to cap it all the flat was bloody filthy. Arif hadn't bothered to clean up. The carpet was littered with empty soft drink cans. Clothes he'd worn and discarded lay strewn all over the couch. A stack of dirty dishes cluttered the small sink. I told him to open the window to get rid of the disgusting smell of rotting food. He didn't seem to hear me. When I said that the flat was no better than a pig sty, he gave me a filthy look and demanded whether I was a Government Health Inspector. Sarcastic git!

There was a kind of anger about him as black as the hair on his head. I wanted to see his cheeky grin, hear a word or two spoken in jest. God alone knows why I was feeling guilty for what had happened to him. Maybe I'd lost all of my marbles. Since when had Arif's life been of any concern to me?

Deciding not to beat about the bush, I informed him I'd not come to make trouble. All I wanted to know was if he was prepared to swallow his pride and make peace with his dad. Disgust made him scowl. I knew I'd asked the wrong question. Arif almost bit my head off.

I was pleased to see all the fight hadn't left him. There was still some of the old Arif lurking about after all. He told me, after a lot of prodding, what had happened. Kashmir had been shipped off to India. Arif didn't know where she was. There was no way he could get in touch with her. Her younger brother, Kuldip, had told Arif his parents had sent a letter to India, in which they'd made it quite clear Kashmir was to be married off as soon as possible. She was to remain in India. Arif was tearing his hair out, but he'd had the goodness to admit Kashmir was in trouble because of him. Many guys wouldn't do that. It's always easier to let the girl take all of the blame!

Trying to be smart, I suggested he go out to India and bring her back. Arif told me not to be stupid. Didn't I know that India was a big country and he'd merely be wasting his time? Talk about adopting a defeatist attitude.

Arif didn't take too kindly to my blaming him for everything. I told him Kashmir would still be going out with him if he'd been more careful. Because he'd strutted around like a demented peacock, showing off in front of his rat-bag mates, everyone had found out.

Arif didn't like being put in his place by me, a mere female. He told me it took two to tango. I hadn't compared their relationship to a dance! Arif was a big-headed fool, he wanted everything his own way and wasn't prepared to compromise. He didn't know, or nobody had bothered to

70

inform him, that what you wanted and what you got were two completely different faces of a coin. Life was an uphill struggle, he wasn't prepared to do any hard work.

'What you need, Arif, is a good kick in the pants.'

A comical look appeared on his face. Laughter erupted from his mouth and he thumped me on the back. I'd managed to get him into a better frame of mind and thought I'd grab the chance while I had it. 'Arif, I'm going to Pakistan.' I didn't look directly at him as I filled the sink with hot water.

'What!'

'You heard me.' I deliberately rattled the dirty dishes and scraped them clean.

'But why?'

'Our gran's ill and she wants to see me.'

'Who the hell told you that?'

'Your dad.'

Arif slammed his fist down hard on the table. 'I knew it,' he hissed. 'What's his bloody game?'

'It's no game, Sammy wrote a letter. She's in trouble. I agreed to go out.'

'You've got a screw loose, woman!' he raved.

'No, I haven't.'

'You can't go. Don't let my dad force you into something you'll regret later on.'

'Stop being so bloody melodramatic. I made a promise and I intend to keep it.'

He wanted to know who was going with me. When I said I was going on my own, he told me I couldn't. It wasn't safe for me to travel alone. I tried not to give the game away by refusing to listen to him. Telling him I had things to do, I headed for the door.

'Hang on a minute, Stacey, I'll go with you.' He'd saved me the grovelling. Containing my delight was difficult.

'Don't be silly, you can't go with me.'

'Stop acting big, Stacey. Dad isn't going so I might as well tag along.'

'You're being ridiculous, Arif. I'm quite capable of taking care of myself.'

'I'd like to go, Stacey, there's nothing for me here. To tell you the truth I could do with a change of scenery. But there are conditions.'

'What conditions?'

'First of all,' he stated arrogantly, 'I know Dad put you up to this.'

'That's rubbish!' I lied. 'He did no such thing.'

'Liar,' he drawled, 'why else would you come to see me? You little sneak!'

'Okay, so it was his idea. He won't let me go alone.'

'Learn to tell the truth, Stacey dear. It won't kill you to be honest once in a while!'

'Look, I'm sorry for messing you about. Are you prepared to go with me? Just give me a straight answer!'

'It would serve you right if I refused. Tell that meddling fool I want nothing to do with him, but he can pay for my ticket 'cause I'm skint.'

'Fine,' I snapped, 'I'll tell him,' then sauntered out chuckling.

Part Two

Trouble Abroad

Arif and I said our farewells and boarded the National Express coach that would take us to London. Bagging the seat nearest the window, I made myself as comfortable as possible.

Arif slumped down beside me. 'Do me a favour Stacey, wake me up when London's in sight.'

What fantastic company I was taking with me. Resigning myself to the fact I had no other choice but to put up with Arif's boring presence for the next two weeks, I took a look at the other passengers. There weren't many. An elderly couple in front of us had already unpacked their lunch and were busy tucking in. Somewhere at the back a baby bawled its head off. A little brat kept darting up and down the aisle. A hearty slap sent him sulking to his seat, where he sat with the most fantastic scowl on his chubby little face. If nothing else, I had the time to mull over the events leading to our departure.

Aunt Razia had thanked me for my help, not that I'd done anything yet. 'Give this money to Sameena,' she'd whispered, 'just do not let anybody else see it.' She'd placed a roll of what looked like monopoly money into my hand.

'Is there anything you'd like me to say to Sammy?'

'Tell her that I am sorry. I can do nothing.'

I put the money into my purse, kissed her and told her I'd see her as soon as I got back. There seemed to be nothing but misery working in our family. Everyone had their own bitter battle raging on unnoticed.

At the Interchange I had experienced a pang of sorrow for Uncle Naveed. I could tell he'd wanted to say something to Arif. But Arif, the arrogant devil, hadn't even looked in his dad's direction. It looked like his pride was more important to him. Life was too short to waste on petty squabbles. But if Arif and his dad wanted to despise each other, that was their problem.

A slight twinge of apprehension had begun to make me feel edgy. Only a fool would have undertaken the mission I'd set out for. I was a fool! I'd no idea what would be waiting for me when we got to Karachi. How would I communicate with the family? I couldn't speak a word of Urdu. The relatives I'd never seen were bound to expect something from me. Only time would tell.

My main concern was whether or not Dad's family would take to me. Settling back with a copy of 'Smash Hits', I read it to pass the time. In my opinion long journeys are really dull. I wished that I could get to my destination without having to take any form of public transport. Wouldn't it be great if we could jump up in the air and land in another country?

Warm sunshine and the motion of the moving coach lulled me eventually into sleep. I must have slept for hours. The smell of coffee woke me up.

'Come on, sleepy head,' Arif said. 'Rise and shine.' He appeared to be in a better frame of mind.

'Thanks,' I grunted. 'How much longer to go?'

'Ten minutes. Come on, drink it while it's hot.'

The coach was beginning to slow down. Jumping up like an excited kid, Arif said, 'Pakistan here I come!'

Sitting for so long had cramped my legs and I'd got pins and needles in my left foot. Arif, the perfect gentleman, had already bounded to the front of the coach and was stretching lazily.

'I feel as stiff as a corpse,' I grumbled.

He replied, 'Pull a comb through your hair woman. I don't want you showing me up.'

'Aw shut up. It'd take more than me to show up a nerd like you.'

Once all our luggage was checked in at the airport, we had a long wait. Arif and I sat down in the waiting room. 'I hate all this delay.'

'Take it easy, Stacey. We'll be on our way soon. Shall I get you a drink?'

I shook my head, 'Don't bother.'

Sulkily, I sat down and decided to study the hundreds of people rushing about like headless chickens. When our call came, I rushed to my feet and swung my handbag over my shoulder. Arif ducked his head and said, 'Watch it. You almost hit me!'

'Sorry!' I grinned. 'Come on, shake a leg, it's time to go.'

The river of people flowed slowly. Everybody was heading in the same direction. The sheer size of the plane threw me into a state of panic. Never having travelled in one before, I allowed all sorts of thoughts to flash through my mind. What if the plane crash landed? What if it got blown out of the sky? Stupid twit, I cursed. Why are you risking your neck in this tin bucket that may never touch solid ground. What a terrible mistake I was making. I was a bit pessimistic. Nobody wants to die and I most certainly had no desire to have my life extinguished like a flame.

Arif pulled his wallet out of his jacket and took out a photograph of Kashmir. She was smiling radiantly. 'I wonder how she is,' he pondered. 'Listen Stacey, there's something I have to tell you.' A sheepish look appeared on his face. 'The reason I agreed to travel with you was because I had an ulterior motive. When you're safe and sound, I'm leaving Pakistan.'

'What?' I stared at him in disbelief.

'I have to find Kashmir. I can't rest until I know she's alright.'

'Arif, you can't be serious!'

'I'm deadly serious, so don't bother trying to talk me out of it. This is one thing I've got to do. I'm going to take a plane from Lahore to New Delhi, and then I'm going to find her!'

'You're out of your tiny mind. What about me?'

'Stacey, you're old enough to look after yourself. Before I agreed to come out here, you were prepared to travel on your own. Don't worry I'll hang around for a few days. Then after that I'm off.'

'Suit yourself,' I retorted flatly. 'If you want to go, it's up to you.'

'Thanks for your support, Stacey,' he snapped sarcastically. 'I really appreciate it.' He gulped his Pepsi noisily.

'Can I come with you?'

'Sorry! I really had to squeeze Kuldip to find out where Kashmir is. She's living outside New Delhi in a village called Chandipur. I've managed to get the address.'

'Where's the money for a ticket coming from?'

Smiling triumphantly, he said, 'Mum lent me it.'

'I can't believe you'd scrounge from her. Have you no pride?'

'Pride doesn't come into it. I'll pay her back.'

Reluctantly, I gave in. 'If you're so desperate, then you should go.'

He had tricked me into believing his concern had been for my welfare alone.When all the time he was only on this wild goose chase for Kashmir!

Relief washed over me as the plane touched down.My feet were killing me. Staring down at the swollen flesh that refused to fit into my sandals, I informed Arif I needed to freshen up. I turned on the tap, washed my face and sponged my feet with a paper towel. I didn't look too bad!

Arif walked with a fresh bounce, the long journey hadn't bothered him at all. Cramp made my legs shake. As I got ready to follow Arif down the plane steps, the intense heat hit me. A light-headed feeling enveloped me, the warm air seemed to climb into my clothes. Turning to see if I was following, Arif smiled. I didn't return his friendly gesture.

Grabbing hold of my wrist, he helped to guide me. His hands were sweaty. The feeling made me feel sick so I pulled away.

'What's up Stacey?'

'Don't touch me, it's too hot.'

'For someone whose gob is always on full throttle, you're really quiet.'

'I'd no idea it'd be so bloody scorching!' Sweat trickled down my face.

'You haven't seen anything yet, just wait until the sun comes up.'

Arif was in his element.The heat and noise didn't bother him at all.Unaware of my discomfort he strolled along without a care in the world.

'Hey Stacey, there's something I have to tell you.'

Silently, I groaned. I wasn't in the mood for his childish games.

'You're at my mercy, all alone in a strange country.You don't know the natives or their language, and you have to depend on me for almost everything.'

It had never occurred to me Arif might try something stupid. He couldn't help it.

'I'm not about to fall for that! You try anything underhand and I'll never forgive you.'

He laughed. 'Little fool, I'm winding you up.'

'Piss off, Arif!'

'Come on, woman, relax. A monkey's got more of a sense of humour than you.'

'Don't keep talking about yourself!'

We piled our luggage on a trolley and passed through customs, where everything was checked by a stern-faced officer. Outside the airport, people stood behind a huge steel barrier. Somebody from our family was bound to be amongst them. A man with skin the colour of roast chestnut sauntered over to join us. I thought he was a relative. Speaking to Arif, he motioned towards the trolley. Arif shook his head and the man reluctantly went his way.

'What did he want?'

'To offer his services, by the time we get out of here we'll get hounded by plenty more of his type.'

He didn't look very happy. I scanned the crowds of people. It looked like there was nobody amongst them remotely aware of us.

'Stacey, didn't your mum say there'd be someone here to meet us?'

'Yeah, an Uncle Ali.'

'Well, it looks like he's forgotten!'

I found it impossible to offer an articulate reply. He couldn't have forgotten us. I'd seen Uncle Naveed sending a telegram over the 'phone to his sister.There had to be some other explanation! Arif was tight-lipped and quiet. I went over to a row of benches and sat down. Checking his wallet for change, he hurried off to find a 'phone. Having no desire to get up and follow him, I remained where I was. My feet were so swollen, it was a relief to take the weight off them.

I had a chance to look around. There was a strong smell of spice in the air. People rushed in and out of the airport, others made their way towards the taxi stands. It's difficult to explain but I felt weird.We'd been stranded, not a very comforting feeling, especially after a long journey. Sitting back with my feet resting on the luggage trolley, I watched the sun creep up.The sky was an artist's palette of soft pinks and oranges, crushed copper merged with silver to give the most spectacular sunrise I'd ever seen.

A young girl wearing a tattered dress approached me, her feet were bare and the duppatta around her neck was full of holes. She stretched out her hand, gazed up at me, and her thin face was tear-stained and dirty.

'What is it?' I asked.

She didn't reply. Her stare was now fixed firmly on my handbag. Try again, said a voice inside my head. The poor kid must have sensed I wasn't a good samaritan. Dragging her feet, she moved on and stopped a young couple. The man gave her a coin. The sight of that kid begging moved me deeply. I didn't know that sort of thing really existed.That's a pretty lame excuse considering all the poverty in Pakistan, but I'd never seen anything like it close to before.

The strain of sitting in the sun was taking its toll. A slow, throbbing pain worked its way into my skull and nagged away until my head felt ready to explode. Something fell into my lap. A huge mosquito flapped about aimlessly. It nearly gave me a heart attack! I shook it off my dress. It fell to the ground where it promptly met with a nasty accident.

They were all over the place. I swatted them with my hands and wished that Arif would hurry up. Just when I thought I couldn't take any more, Arif showed up. I seized his arm. 'Thank God, you're back.Come on, let's get out of here. I've been eaten alive!'

'Calm down.What's the worst they can do to you?'

Talk about being sympathetic! 'This place stinks.Why the hell did you take so long?'

'I've been trying to get in touch with Uncle Ali. He'll be on his way now. Dad didn't send a telegram!'

'That's a load of rubbish. I was there when he sent it.'

'Uncle Ali just told me he had no idea we were coming.'

'Arif, I know what I saw! Your dad wouldn't trick us.'

'Yes, he would Stacey! Open your eyes, girl. Dad's not the hero you've made him into. I know how his mind works and I also know what a cunning devil he can be!'

'The only reason you're having a go at him is because of Kashmir. If you ask me, you got what you deserve!'

He was angry. He pushed the trolley over to the taxi-stand and leaned against it. If he wanted to sulk, then that was up to him! He was crying out for a smack in the teeth.

Sweat trickled down my back and made my clothes cling to my body. I was already having my regrets. What had I let myself in for?

A green van pulled up and a stocky man with a dusting of grey in his otherwise black hair got out. He walked with a slight limp. 'I am so sorry that you wait for me, I had important work to finish.' He embraced Arif and patted me on the head like you would a little kid.

Uncle Ali drove us to a mountainous area where all the land was green.The trees were heavy with fruit, and cattle grazed lazily in the hot summer sun. I held my seat with both hands as the van bobbed up and down on the rough dirt road. At the top of the mountain was a scattering of white-washed houses. Uncle Ali pointed his out to us. 'That one, it has the green gate.'

His English was broken, but I had to give him his due. At least he made the effort!

Arif took the luggage out of the boot. My body ached from sitting for so long. 'I could do with a good, long soak in the bath.' I remarked.

Arif grinned and turned away.What the hell was so funny?

'You better get used to real life Stacey. You won't get any hot baths here.All the water has to be collected from the waterfalls and that'll be your job.'

'Oh, shut up!'

Uncle Ali knocked on the gate. The steady sound of footsteps slapping on the ground let us know we'd been heard.

Arif, struggling with the suitcases, glanced my way. If he thought I was going to help him, he was very much mistaken. It was about time he did some work, the lazy git!

A small woman resembling Uncle Naveed bid us follow her into the house. Hugging Arif, she spoke quickly and also welcomed me with a tight embrace, the last thing I needed. Bright-coloured clothes flapped on the line in the huge yard. Half a dozen chickens scratched around, eyeing us from time to time with lopsided looks.

The interior of the house was amazing considering the condition of the streets outside. Aunt Zakia led us into a spacious room. A ceiling fan buzzed noisily overhead. Directly in front of us were two large shuttered windows. Arif pulled them open. A blue and white rug covered the tiled floor. Uncle Ali told us to sit down. 'You are tired, first we eat and then you rest.'

That sounded ideal. Aunt Zakia smiled at me on her way out of the room.

'I can't wait to see Sammy,' I said as I sat down. 'We've got a lot to catch up with.'

'Women! All you ever do is talk a load of bull.' He bent down to unlace his shoes. I wanted to give him a kick.

Sarcastically, I said, 'This place is full of action, where is everybody?'

Flopping down on the bed, Arif smirked. 'They all ran for the hills when they found out we were coming.' Aunt Zakia returned carrying a tray with two long glasses of juice. I took mine gratefully and gulped it down. She spoke to Arif in a good-natured manner. They appeared to be getting on quite well until Arif mentioned Sameena.

Aunt Zakia pulled a face and muttered something which made Arif flush with rage. I found myself wishing I could understand what was being said. It wasn't very polite to keep interrupting just so I could find out what was going on!

Aunt Zakia waved her fat arms about as though she was directing traffic. A splutter of laughter erupted from my mouth. Arif shot me a poisonous look. I'd been hoping to catch forty winks, but that expectation was dashed when Arif got to his feet. 'Get your stuff, Stacey, we're leaving!'

'Steady on. We only just got here.'

'Don't get comfortable. The sooner we leave the better.'

'What's going on?'

Brushing away a fly, he said, 'Don't ask questions, just do as I tell you.'

Digging my heels in, I shook my head. 'I'm not going anywhere until you tell me what's going on!'

Sighing angrily, he pulled me to my feet.

Aunt Zakia intervened. She spoke shrilly. Arif ignored her.

'We can't leave yet,' I reminded him.'We came out here to see our sick grandmother!'

'Well, that's tough. She died nine days ago.'

'Oh, my God! There must be some sort of mistake. How come nobody bothered to tell us?'

'Shut up! I can't believe you actually agreed to come out here in the first place. This is all your bloody fault.'

'That's great, go on blame me. You didn't have to tag along. How dare you winge? At least you got a free holiday! If you want to leave, you can. But I intend to stay right here. I've got things to do!'

Frustration made Arif's face turn red. 'Listen, you stubborn cow, you don't know anything about this place.What have you got to do?'

'I'm not leaving, Arif, not until I get to see Dad's grave. Coming out here might have been a waste of time for you but it isn't for me.You're going to take me to his grave. Then I might consider leaving!'

Bursting with annoyance, he caught hold of my arm. 'If I take you, will you promise to leave with me?'

I nodded.

'Good, now come on!' He walked quickly out into the courtyard.Over his shoulder, he said, 'This bloody dump hasn't changed that much since I was here last.'

Aunt Zakia followed us slowly. She mopped the tears from her face with the corner of her duppatta.

Arif led me out into the garden. The ground was soft underfoot. A handful of plants grew in untidy clumps. Pointing to the lime tree, he said, 'It's over there, Stacey. Go on. I won't come with you.'

My heart thumped painfully in my breast. For some unknown reason my mouth had gone dry. I came to a standstill by the tiny graveyard which was sectioned off with a crude wire fence. The headstones all looked the same to me. 'Which one is it, Arif?'

'The one in the middle.'

Kneeling down I stared at the grave through a film of tears. A crow cawed rudely in the tree above. That same raw ache I'd experienced when Dad died returned to haunt me once again. 'Dad, I miss you so much,' I whispered.'I know you can't hear me. I just wish you were still alive.You wouldn't believe what a mess my life's in at the moment.'

'Stacey, come on. Let's go!'

Arif was getting impatient. I needed more time to lay all my ghosts to rest. I ignored him and remained where I was.

The soft rustle of material distracted me. A hand rested gently on my shoulder. 'Hi, Stacey, how are you?'

'Sammy, it's good to see you.' I hugged her.

'I'm sorry to bother you. Go on. Sit back down.'

'The writing, Sammy, what does it say? I can't see my dad's name anywhere.'

Pointing to the third row of writing, she said,'It's written in Urdu. You won't be able to understand it.'

'Are you sure it's the right one? I don't trust that rat-bag!'

Sameena nodded like a wise old woman. 'Trust me, Stacey.'

I turned to Arif, 'Give me the camera.'

'What for?'

'To take some snaps, you fool.' I snatched it from his hand and stepped back in order to get a clearer shot. 'Mum would like to see what Dad's grave looks like.'

'Hurry up, Stacey!'

'Get lost, Arif, I need more time.'

Sameena took him into her house. As a parting shot, he said, 'Don't use all the film.'

'There's another roll in my suitcase. Just go away.'

It was difficult to analyse the thoughts going through my head. Dad had been so much more than just a dad! He'd been my best friend. It'd always been easier for me to talk things through with him.Mum had always been too wrapped up in Granddad's needs to ever care about me. After all these years I was by his side again but in a different sort of way. I still loved him, years of grieving had not bridged that intense feeling. If only he could get up and talk with me. There was so much I had to tell him, so many things to discuss. The sun burnt the back of my neck. Flies buzzed around my face persistently and the smell from an open drain made my stomach churn.

'Stacey, come inside. You'll get sun stroke if you stay out too long,' called Sameena.

As I got to my feet, my head began to spin, my mouth filled with salty water and I felt sick. Swaying dangerously, I stumbled and hugged the tree. Sameena cried out and ran to my side.

'Arif, come and give me a hand, Stacey's not well.'

Groaning as green lights flashed before my eyes, I managed to mumble, 'Don't worry, I'll be fine. Just take me inside.'

Arif carried me into the house and put me down on the bed. Sameena ran off to fetch some water. 'Here, get this down you. It might help.'

My stomach heaved and without any warning I threw up all over a very horrified Arif. 'Oh my God, I feel awful.'

'The feeling's mutual,' he agreed as he stepped back. 'You could have told me you wanted a bucket!'

Sameena sniggered, 'Go into the washroom and clean up.'

Arif wrinkled his nose in disgust. 'It's bloody typical of you, Stacey. I swear you've got it in for me.'

Sameena pushed him playfully. 'Come on, move out.I'll have to clean up before Umar gets back.'

'I'm sorry, Sammy. I'll do it.'

'No, it's okay. You get some rest.'

'I've got so much to tell you,' I said sleepily. 'But it'll have to wait. All I want now is to get some kip.'

Closing my eyes, I drifted off into a restless state of sleep. The noise from the ceiling-fan invaded my dreams.

It was dark when I woke up. Arif and Sameena sat in a corner of the dimly lit room and talked in hushed tones. Having no desire to eavesdrop, I said, 'What time is it? I'm hungry.'

Arif came towards the bed and grinned. 'We've been waiting for you to catch up on your beauty sleep and now that you're awake, we can go up to the other house.'

The night air was warm, insects buzzed noisily in the trees. A firefly passed us as we walked by. Everything seemed so peaceful, no loud music nor wild parties. No car horns honking loudly. No sign of civilisation anywhere.

Aunt Zakia gave us a frosty reception. I didn't blame her, not after the rude way we'd departed from her house. Without speaking, she placed large plates of rice and chicken in front of us. Arif pulled a face behind her back and whispered, 'Crabby old cow.'

I spluttered and in the process almost choked to death on a bone. 'You're crazy.' Arif gave me a thump on the back.

Uncle Ali came and sat down with us on the floor. He smiled at Sameena, she flushed and averted her eyes.

'You feel better now?' he observed the way I fed my face.

'Yeah, much better. It must have been the long journey. I was really tired.'

'And stupid,' Arif added.'You could have gone to the graveyard later on.'

'What's it to you, Arif?' Sameena defended me.

'She's careless,' he replied as he chewed a piece of meat. 'If she gets ill, we'll have to look after her.'

Uncle Ali nodded in agreement. I didn't like the way Arif talked about me. He acted as though I wasn't present. 'Listen here, Florence Nightingale, don't talk over me! In case you haven't noticed, I'm here.'

Sameena laughed softly. 'You two, honestly. You're always at each other's throats.'

'He bloody gets on my nerves!' I snapped.

'Aw, shut up Stacey.'

Uncle Ali, unable to keep up with us, got up and walked away.

'Listen, guys, you'll have to sleep here tonight. There isn't enough room in my hovel.'

'How come you're living in such a dump?' Arif asked rudely.

'Beggars can't be chosers! I've got no choice.'

'Sammy, why didn't you write and tell us that the old girl kicked the bucket?'

'I did!'

'Yeah, sure you did. Your dad would have told me if he'd got a letter.'

'Don't give me that rubbish!' she exploded, 'every week since I've been here, I've been writing letters to you guys. And none of you bothered to reply.'

Arif shook his head. 'We never got those letters Sameena.'

Aunt Zakia carried in a tray of sliced fruit and placed it on the floor. Speaking to Sameena loudly, she gestured towards the door. Sameena got to her feet and left the room.

'What was all that about?'

'Her husband wants her. I don't think Sameena's happy here, Stacey. Did you see that bruise on her arm?'

I shook my head. 'How come she isn't living here with the rest of the family? This house is big enough for them all. I know Sammy's hiding something from us. I'll find out later on.'

Sameena didn't return. Arif got up and stretched. 'I could do with a sleep. What about you?'

'Later on. I'm going to have a wash and then I'll go and see Sammy.'

'I wouldn't do that if I were you! Wait until the morning.'

'Why?'

'Because our Uncle and Aunt will think it strange that you've gone for a walk in the middle of the night.'

84

'Okay, you win!'

'I'll see you tomorrow,' he scratched his arm. 'Bloody mosquitoes, they really bite.'

'You'll live.' I replied remembering how he'd mocked me at the airport.

Aunt Zakia showed me to my room. I had to share with her daughter Shakila.The water in the tank was cold. Gritting my teeth, I washed my face and neck. My feet were still aching and the cold water helped to relieve the pain.

A young girl with long brown hair and green eyes sat on the bed. She smiled at me as I stepped out of the washroom. 'You are Steecey?' she asked. I liked the way she pronounced my name.

'That's right.Who are you?'

'I am your cousin, Shakila.Where is Arif?'

'He's gone to bed!'

'You look like your father,' she told me. 'He was a good man.'

'Did you know him?'

Shakila shook her head. 'My mother told me all about him. I have his photographs.'

I nodded.

'No school in the morning. I am glad you came. I want to meet Arif.'

She had mentioned that idiot twice, I found it strange she was so eager to see someone she'd never met before. Something wasn't quite right.

'Hey, Shakila, how come Sammy lives on her own?'

'You speak too quickly. It is difficult for me to understand you.'

'Why is Sameena living by herself? This house is very big!'

She nodded her head. 'My brother Umar, he is no good!'

She had my full attention. 'Tell me more.'

'There is not much to tell. Umar has some very bad friends and he spends time with them.'

'What about Sammy? She shouldn't be living by herself!'

'That is what my mother said. Umar will not listen. He likes to give trouble.'

'When did our grandmother die?'

'Not very long time, she wanted to see you.'

It wasn't my fault she'd decided not to wait for us. Sameena's state worried me. It wasn't right she had to put up with an ignorant husband.

Making a mental note to discuss things with Arif, I unpacked my case and got ready for bed. Shakila didn't have very much to say, I watched her as she tied her hair back and climbed into her bed. She said goodnight, turned over and closed her eyes.

I switched off the light, lay in the dark room and thought things over. Sameena had been desperate when she'd written to her dad begging him to send me over. And now that I was here, she showed no apparent signs of distress.

What sort of a man was her husband? I was going to find out what was going on and I didn't care who got hurt in the process.

The sun was shining brightly when Aunt Zakia called us to breakfast. Shakila was in the washroom so I had to wait. Pulling a comb through my hair, I paced the room. Shakila stepped out in a cloud of perfume, she had tied her hair up in a bun and wore a beautiful green and pink suit.

'I will see you later,' she said before leaving the room.

Closing the door behind me, I washed my face and cleaned my teeth. I didn't bother with any make up. Somebody banged rudely on the door. Cursing, I opened it to find Arif standing outside. 'Hi, how are you?'

'Same as last night,' I replied. 'What's the hurry?'

'There's no hurry, I just thought I'd wait for you. Are you ready?'

'Yeah. Have you met Shakila?'

Arif nodded. A grin spread across his face. 'She's really something.'

'She's not your type,' I said spitefully.

'And you are?'

'I never said that! She was dying to meet you last night.What gives?'

Arif shrugged. 'Don't know. She just seems like a nice girl.'

Shakila couldn't do enough for Arif. Pouring his tea, she set it in front of him on the table. 'You want sugar, Arif?'

'Yeah, two please.' He was enjoying all the attention.

'I will get your breakfast for you now.' She walked off. Her hips moved up and down. I knew she was doing it on purpose. Arif laughed loudly. 'Did you see her?'

'Yeah, she fancies you, Arif.'

Arif scowled.'Don't be stupid, Stacey. Like you said, she's not my type.'

'Shut up, here she comes.'

Breakfast over, I made my way to Sameena's house. She was sitting in the yard washing dishes.

'Hey Sammy, how's life?'

She managed a rather watery smile and began scrubbing a saucepan with a small rag and some sand. Terrible anger rose inside me. She was being forced to live like a primitive while those around her lived like royalty. 'Sammy, have you got any money?'

'What's that? I've forgotten what the stuff looks like!'

'Listen, we need to talk.'

'Sit down. I've got work to do. You can talk while I get on with it.'

'Sammy, your mum misses you. Are you coming back with us or are you gonna live in this dump in the middle of nowhere?'

A strange look appeared on her face. 'I can't go home now, Stacey.' Pouring water onto the ground, she swept it away with a broom.

'Why not?'

'Things have changed. I've decided to stay with Umar.'

'But your letter!'

'I know, Stacey, like I said things have changed. I can't go back to Bradford now.'

It was clear she had no desire to discuss her plans with me. 'Look around you, Sammy. This place isn't for you. You deserve better than this dump.'

'You try telling that to my dad. I'm here because of him.'

She disappeared into the house and returned with a bundle of clothes and a bar of soap. She tossed the lot to the ground and went to fill a large bowl with water.

'Do you want a hand?'

'No, thanks. I'll have to manage on my own.'

'What's wrong with you? I'm on your side, remember!'

'I'm sorry, Stacey. I'm really fed up. I'd give anything for a bag of fish and chips. I honestly never believed I'd miss Bradford so much. I don't belong here at all.'

'So why not come home with me?'

'Because Umar won't let me. I've got to stay here.'

'This is your life, Sammy. He can't rule it for you. I came all the way out here for you. You could at least have the decency to tell me what's happened to change your mind.'

'If I tell you, will you promise not to tell Arif?'

'Sure thing.'

She scrubbed the clothes with the soap and said. 'When I first got here, everything was great! My in-laws couldn't do enough for me. After the wedding, things really started going downhill. Umar's not at all what I expected him to be. He's greedy, selfish and jealous of me.'

'In what way?' I demanded.

Sameena shrugged her shoulders and changed the water.

'He resents me, Stacey. I'm not what he wants. The only reason he's got me living here against my will is because I'm his ticket to freedom. As long as I'm here, there's a chance he'll get his visa. He's been refused three times now and, I tell you, Stacey, he's desperate to get out of here.'

'Tell him you want to go back home!'

'It's not that simple. Mum and Dad want me to stay here with him.'

'That's not true! Your mum doesn't want anything of the sort. She's really unhappy without you, Sammy.'

I was wasting my time trying to get through to her, she was so upset nothing seemed to click in her head.

She looked at me sadly.'You're only saying that to make me feel better. If they missed me so much, I'd have received at least one letter from them in all the months I've been here.' She shook the clothes angrily and hung them on the line.

'Look, I know you're upset. I would be if I lived here. Believe me, your mum was going out of her head with worry.'

'Don't give me that rubbish, Stacey. I may be stuck out here in the back of beyond, but I'm not bloody stupid.'

'Feeling sorry for yourself isn't going to help. Pack your stuff and we'll leave now.'

'Umar took my passport.'

'What the hell for?' Turning round, we saw Arif standing close by.

'How long have you been listening?' Sameena asked with a scowl on her pretty face.

'Long enough. Where did he put your passport?'

'It's in the suitcase on top of the wardrobe.'

'I'll get it for you,' volunteered Arif.

'No!' she cried. 'Don't do that.'

Arif ignored her and marched into the room.

'Please, Arif, leave it.'

'Are you scared of him?'

Sameena shivered.'You're going to make so much trouble for me, he'll beat me up!'

'I'd like to see him try.' Climbing on the bed, he took a firm hold of the handle.'Move back so I can pull it down.'

The case was locked. 'Have you got a key?' Arif wanted to know.

'Umar's got it.'

'Give me something to break the bloody lock off then.'

'No, Arif, don't.'

'Wait on. I'll give you a knife.' I rummaged around in the plastic bowl full of washed crockery and cutlery. 'I've got one.'

Jamming the blade under the lock, Arif pushed it sideways, the lock snapped. Throwing open the lid, he picked up a bundle of letters tied with a piece of string. 'These yours, Sameena?'

Sheer shock flitted across Sameena's face.

I put my arm around her waist for support and said. 'No wonder, we never got any news from you.'

'I can't believe it. All this time he's been hiding my letters.What a traitor!' She started crying.

'You're coming with us, Sameena,' Arif said angrily.

'I can't ,' she sobbed. 'Umar won't let me. He's got an interview next week with the High Commission and I've got to go with him.'

'Let him go on his own, Sammy.'

'He can't go without me. They want to see me as well.'

'Take my advice, little sister. Get your stuff together and we'll head off to Lahore. Mum's got relatives there who'd love to put us up. I'm not going to sit back and let some guy ruin your life for you.'

'It's too late for that, Arif. I'm expecting a baby.'

'A what?' He asked, stunned by her news.

'You heard her, Arif. One of those horrid, little creatures that cry, and mucky nappies all day long.'

'How the hell did it happen?'

Talk about thick, the guy was so stupid. 'Come on, Arif, surely you've heard about the birds and the bees? Does Sammy have to spell it out to you?'

'You should have been careful,' he snapped.

'What are you, the bloody family planning clinic?' I fumed.

'Please don't squabble. There's enough misery in my life without you two fighting.'

'We're not fighting, Sammy,' I smiled at her. 'You know very well we like to tease each other.'

'At the moment, I don't find anything amusing,' Arif said arrogantly. 'So what are you going to do, Sammy?'

'What do you want me to do ?'

'Knock his teeth down his bloody throat. He's been deceiving you all this time. Doesn't that bother you at all?'

Sameena shrugged and went back out into the yard. 'He's a lot stronger than I am, Arif. I'm no match for him.'

'Well, I am. When does he get home?'

I watched her hang some more clothes on the line. 'He'll come home when he's hungry or when the money runs out. Most nights, I'm on my own here.'

'You're joking!' I exclaimed. 'This place is deserted.'

'Stacey, I wish Mum and Dad had given this marriage some thought before they carted me off to this awful place. I hate it here, there's no running water. I've got no electricity and when the oil for the lamp runs out, I can never buy any because all the money's gone!'

'Can't you live with Aunt Zakia?' I asked. Her predicament worried me so much.

'Umar won't live with them. They had a fight and Uncle Ali threw us out of the house. He told Umar to stay away.'

'That's not fair,' I interjected.'What did he do?'

'He stole the gold that Aunt Zakia had done for Shakila's wedding.'

'What a charmer Dad married you off to.'

'I'm going to have a word with them and tell them to let you move back in. It's not right you live out here.' I was trying to be helpful.

Sameena sat down and looked at us both, sadly. 'Isn't this all so hopeless? I can't believe I was born for this awful day. I wish I could go home.'

Arif put his arm around her and hugged her close. 'Don't worry, Sameena. We'll think of something. If Uncle Ali lets you back into the house, that'll be ideal. But if he refuses, I'm going to get in touch with Mum's sister and tell her to let you live there.'

That seemed to comfort Sameena I couldn't begin to imagine the hardship she'd been forced to endure because of Umar. It wasn't fair on her, Uncle Naveed had sold his daughter to the highest bidder. I intended to have a talk with him when I returned to Bradford. He'd have to get her out of the mess he'd thrown her into.

I'd never realised that the weather could be so hot, the ground under my feet was like an oven. On the way back to the other house, I passed the graveyard. Dad's presence comforted me. It sounded silly and morbid, but that was the feeling I got everytime I sat by his grave.

Later on, Sameena had taken us to the shops. I'd been so embarrassed when she'd bought her food on credit. The shopkeeper had given it to her without asking any questions. The poor girl was a nervous wreck!

Back at the house, I spent some time with Shakila who was busy with a piece of embroidery. She worked quickly and the work she produced was of an excellent standard. 'Who's it for?'

'For my dowry,' she replied. 'When I marry Arif, I will need lots of nice things for my house.'

'Arif! Do you mean our Arif?' I asked, with uncontained surprise.

'Yes, he will be my husband.'

'You seem pretty sure of that.' The urge to kick her rose inside me.

'It has been decided a long time ago. Arif will be very happy with me.'

'You'd better not let him hear you saying that,' I said, controlling the urge to spill the beans about Kashmir. That would show her what had been decided. She was a sneaky little cow!

'My father will discuss the details with Arif when the time is right.' She made it sound like a business transaction.

'If anyone wants me, I'll be in the bedroom.' I said, leaving her to dream about something that was highly unlikely to happen.

I intended to rest for a short while but fell asleep. Voices raised in anger woke me up. Cursing under my breath, I searched around for my sandals. Something skittered past my hand, making my heart jump. There was a shout and the sound of breaking glass. I ran to investigate.

Aunt Zakia stood staring in horror at the fragments of a water set. A man with short hair, dressed in a grey shalvaar and kameez stood watching her. She managed to compose herself and picked up the broom which she brought down on his head. He looked at her in alarm and stepped back. Aunt Zakia shouted at him and threatened to attack again. Shakila stood behind the tree in the garden, her hand over her mouth.

'Who's that?' I asked her.

The man looked my way.

'That is my brother,' she said. 'He wants money.'

'Hey, you,' I approached him. 'What's your game?'

He seemed taken aback and frowned at me. His mother mentioned my dad's name. I didn't like the way he smiled at me. He came forward, holding out a hand.

Just then the door opened and Sameena stepped inside. She stopped in her tracks when she saw Umar. There was a huge bruise over her eye and her top lip was swollen.

'Sammy, what happened to you?' I hurried to her side.

Her eyes filled with tears. 'You'll have to get me out of here, Stacey I can't take many more of his beatings.'

I couldn't believe the way she'd been mistreated. Fury made me see red. 'How dare you hit Sammy?' I screamed at him. 'What gives you the right to batter my best friend?'

I was wasting my time. He couldn't understand me. He walked past me as if I didn't exist and took hold of Sameena's arm. She struggled to free herself. But he held her tight and began hauling her towards the gate.

Sameena cried out to me. 'Stacey, please stop him!'

Acting on the spur of the moment, I jumped on his back and held on. 'Let her go,' I yelled in his ear. 'Take your hands off her!'

Umar released Sameena and, without any difficulty, he threw me to the ground, where I lay with the breath knocked out of me. He was such a gentleman!

'Stacey, are you okay?' Sameena came to my rescue.

'I'm fine, just a bit bruised that's all.'

Aunt Zakia helped me to my feet. She shook her fist at Umar, who stormed out of the yard.

That evening, Uncle Ali and Arif moved all of Sameena's belongings back into the house. I was so mad at Umar, he'd behaved like a caveman!

'At least I'll be able to sleep tonight,' she said as she washed her face. 'Thanks for sticking up for me, Stacey.'

'What's a bruised butt between friends?' I said and we both burst into fits of laughter.

I remembered the roll of money Aunt Razia had given me and took out my purse. 'Here, Sammy, this is for you.'

Her eyes lit up at the sight of the money. 'Where did you get it?'

'Your mum asked me to give it to you. Just don't go giving it away to that money-grabbing husband of yours.'

'I'm going to buy myself some slippers and a new suit with this,' she said happily. 'We'll go shopping in the morning.'

Sameena decided to call it a night and went to bed. I found it difficult to sleep. Leaving the room quietly, I went outside into the garden and sat down under the tree. A rustling noise startled me. 'Who's there?' My heart leapt into my boots.

'It's me, Arif.'

'What the hell are you creeping about for? You scared the life out of me.'

'Keep your voice down, woman. We've got to talk.'

'I'm not stopping you.'

'Stacey, I've decided to go to Lahore. If I'm not back by next Friday, you'll have to head for home on your own.'

'I can't do that!'

'You've got no choice. Please, Stacey, don't make me beg you. Do me a favour and keep an eye on Sameena for me.'

'Arif, you can't go yet. Sammy needs us both to support her.'

'Don't make this harder than it already is. I've got to go now, Stacey. This is the only chance I'm going to get. I've got to take it or I'll spend the rest of my life thinking of what might have been.'

He was so determined to leave. Even though Arif had made his decision a long time ago, I still felt uneasy. 'What if you don't find Kashmir? There's a chance that you never will. What then?'

'I'll come back, I promise. Be a pal, Stacey, take care of Sammy and say my goodbyes for me.'

'You've always taken the easy way out, Arif. You piss me off!'

'Don't forget, if I don't come back on time, go home on your own.' Without any warning, he pulled me into his arms and hugged me. 'I owe you one, Stacey,' he whispered in my ear.

'Good luck, you idiot,' I put on a cheerful face, not wanting to show him my true feelings. Kissing my cheek gently, he disappeared into the night. As I turned to go back to my room, I was certain I saw Shakila hide behind the washroom door.

Everybody wanted to know where Arif was when he didn't show up for breakfast. Shakila glanced at me. The look on her face was one of pure hatred.

'He had to leave,' I said lamely. 'There were some people he wanted to catch up with before going back to England.'

Sameena eyed me questioningly. I prayed she wouldn't put me on the spot. Thankfully, she kept her mouth shut.

As we got ready to go shopping with Uncle Ali, she asked me outright. 'What's the story Stacey? The looks you got at breakfast were anything but friendly.'

'Arif's gone to find Kashmir!' I started to change my clothes.

'Why?'

'Because he loves the girl, isn't that a good enough reason?'

'He never even said goodbye,'she whispered as she combed her hair.

'There wasn't time. He'll be back if he can't find her. I'm sure Shakila was out there last night when we were talking.'

'That doesn't shock me at all,' said Sammy. 'She's got a massive crush on Arif.'

'Here, Sammy is it true she's going to marry Arif?'

Sammy laughed. 'That's a load of bull. Arif wouldn't marry her, but there's no harm in letting her think he will.'

'You should have heard her, she sounded pretty certain.'

Sammy pulled a face. 'She's arrogant, they all bloody are. So when's Arif coming back?'

I shrugged. 'He might not make it back just yet so that means I'll have to go back on my own. What the hell am I going to say to your parents when they ask where Arif is?'

'Tell them the truth,' she said logically. 'It'll teach Dad a good lesson.

He seems to think he'll get his own way all the time. When he finds out Arif tricked him he's not going to be very impressed. But that's his own fault.'

'Do you think Arif will find Kashmir?' I asked seriously.

'I really don't know. I can't understand why he didn't tell me he was going.'

'Don't take it personally. He just thought the fewer people who knew the better. You weren't in the best frame of mind. He didn't want to upset you.'

Sameena eyed me strangely. 'Stacey, do you like Arif?'

'Yeah, why?'

'No reason. It's just he confides in you and I can't understand why. The two of you do nothing but fight.'

I smiled at her. 'We only mess about. I like Arif, but not in the way you think. He's just a mate.'

Our conversation was interrupted by a sulky Shakila. 'My mother is calling you,' she said to Sammy.

'What's up?'

'You have visitors from Lahore.' Turning abruptly, she walked off.

Sammy laughed. 'She's not very happy, is she?'

'Serves her bloody right.' I sniggered.

The relatives from Lahore stayed for three days and then insisted I spend the remainder of my holiday with them. I agreed readily and went to pack my stuff. Sammy watched me enviously. 'I wish I could go with you.'

'Nobody's stopping you, come on.'

'Umar won't let me!'

'Just come!'

After giving it some thought, she hurried off to pack. It wasn't long before we were ready to go. Aunt Zakia and Shakila looked quite annoyed. 'You are very ungrateful,' said Shakila.

'Shut up, Shakila!' hissed Sammy. 'These people are my mum's relatives and I don't see why we shouldn't go with them.'

'Have you asked Umar for his permission?'

'Don't be silly. You know very well he hasn't been home since last night. Tell him I got sick of hanging around and decided to take off.'

I don't think Shakila understood what Sammy said to her. She frowned and stood back watching us. Thanking Aunt Zakia for putting up with me, I handed my bags to Uncle Akram, Aunt Razia's brother-in-law. Sammy got into the van and grinned at me.

'I'm coming in a minute,' I told her. 'There's someone I forgot to say 'bye to.'

I hurried back into the house, I made my way out into the graveyard. The weather was slightly cooler. The sky had turned grey and huge clouds had gathered. Sitting down by Dad's grave, I said, 'Well, Dad, this is it.' I ran my fingertips across his tombstone. 'Oh, Dad, I still miss you so much. All my life I've clung to your memory.'

'Come on, Stacey,' shouted Sameena, who'd followed me.

I dashed the tears from my eyes and stood up, 'I'm coming.' I swallowed. The lump in my throat was choking me.

'Everyone says I'm selfish but I love you Dad. I wish you were still around. 'Goodbye Dad. I'll come back one day.' Without looking at the grave, I hurried back to the van where Uncle Ali was waiting. I thanked him for his hospitality and got in beside Sameena.

The drive was long and Uncle Akram, stopped in a small city, Haripur. Uncle Akram told us Haripur was Pakistan's main supplier of telephone sets and the farmers grew crops which were popular all over the country. The part we saw was very green, the vegetation seemed to thrive in the warm climate.

After a bite to eat, we set off for Islamabad, the capital city. Neat, clean streets and red-bricked houses with sloping roofs reminded me of Leeds. All of officialdom lived and worked in Islamabad. Government offices, the British High Commission and many more to boot. By the time we got to Lahore, it was dark. The air was alive with all sorts of sounds. Car horns blared, people and music coming from the shops spilled out into the night. I was amazed to see how busy the streets were so late at night. All the shops were open and people were strolling about. Aunt Razia's sister, Nilum, greeted us with warm hugs and sent us off to wash before we had our supper. Sammy could barely stay awake. Yawning noisily, she asked to be excused.

I felt a little bit left out as I watched my cousins sitting around chatting amongst each other. They smiled at me but found it difficult to communicate. Aunt Nilum showed me to my room and I fell asleep thinking about Bradford.

The last few days of my holiday flew by. Uncle Akram saw to it that we had a good time. Lahore was beautiful and there was plenty to visit. All the historic buildings such as the old mosques, parks and museums were there. Aunt Nilum explained to me through Sammy that fashion and clothes in Lahore were highly influenced by Indian culture, all the best designed garments were introduced in Islamabad first and then went on to the rest of the country. She took us shopping in the busy bazaars and we got to see for ourselves. I'd never seen so many clothes in my life, they were beautifully decorated with sequins, beads and threadwork.

Aunt Nilum bought me a pair of toe-wedge slippers which had embroidery all over them. I thanked her and we chose a suit to take back home. I liked her, she was warm and friendly and had eyes like Aunt Razia's. She insisted on buying presents for me. I found it was pointless arguing and let her go mad in the shops.

Uncle Akram took Sammy and me to see the Tarbela Dam. What a sight that was! The roar of the water was deafening as it thundered down to meet the river below. I found it hard to believe that men had built it, it was so big and fantastically designed.

Saturday came around and I was ready to leave. I dreaded the tearful farewells and found myself thinking about Arif for the first time since I'd arrived in Lahore. He hadn't been in touch and I was worried about explaining where he was to everyone in Bradford!

Aunt Nilum made breakfast, not that I felt like eating. Sammy hovered about and reminded me I'd come out to Pakistan to see if I could help her go back home. Guilt made me uneasy. It was alright for me. I'd be home soon and would carry on taking everyone and everything for granted. But what about Sammy? How long would it be before she got to see her mum and dad again?

The boys - Aunt Nilum had four - wanted to go to the airport with us. Sammy declined my invitation and said she wasn't feeling well. 'Give this to Mum,' she said. 'Tell her to write, I'll be waiting.'

I put the letter in my handbag and hugged her. 'Take care, Sammy, I'll try my best to talk to your dad for you.'

'It'll be a waste of time,' she sobbed. 'He'll never listen.'

I couldn't say more, she was so upset. Hugging Aunt Nilum, I promised to give the presents she'd packed in my cases to Aunt Razia. All that remained was to get into the waiting van. It was hard to turn away from Sammy, I was deserting her. 'Write to me Sammy and if you ever need anything don't be shy, just ask me!'

She nodded and went into the house.

The flight was tiring and long and I was relieved to be back in Britain. After 'phoning Mum from the airport, I waited for my coach. I wished that I'd got wings so I could fly over the traffic and get home. I was happy to see Bradford again. I'd only been away for two weeks yet everything looked so different. The colours were dull compared to Pakistan where the hot weather and brightly coloured shops and clothes created a mood of liveliness which wasn't evident back in Yorkshire.

There was an uproar when I turned up without Arif. Uncle Naveed almost went through the roof when he found out he'd been tricked. Promising to talk later, I insisted on having a shower and getting some sleep. I was due to start work next morning. Nothing can beat your own bed, I told myself as I stretched lazily and closed my eyes. I fell asleep with Arif on my mind and dreamt he was kissing me! Yuck, what a nightmare!

PART THREE

Trouble in t' Mill

I'm waiting outside the office here at Rhodes and Company. It's been a year since I came to work here and now they're about to give me the boot, sack, call it what you like. After today, I'll be parting ways with the insufferable Morris and his secretary, Cindy. Maybe I'm being slightly dramatic! I'm not really getting sacked, we're merely trying to come to a mutual agreement which doesn't involve court cases and law suits.

I can't believe my bloody luck! How come I get all the hassles? This time I swear it's not my fault. It's all due to Morris and his big ego, the stupid prat.

You're probably wondering just who Morris is. Well, wonder no more, he's the boss's son; which makes him the manager. This enables him to kick all his staff about. Let me tell you what happened after I got back from Pakistan.

Mum and I were arguing all the time over petty things. I was glad to have the job to fall back on. Mum was upset, she'd been hoping my visit to Pakistan would clear up my itchy feet syndrome. But it seemed to get worse. I found I didn't want to be anywhere near my family, especially when Uncle Naveed refused to pay for Sammy's ticket home.

A week after my arrival in Bradford, Sammy took a fall and lost the baby! I was convinced it hadn't been an accident. In my mind, I was certain that Umar was to blame. All my attempts to get in touch with Sammy proved futile. She never replied to any of my letters.

If nobody else in our family was bothered about her silence, I was! I'd seen how she'd been forced to live and decided as soon as I had enough money, I'd buy a ticket for her. Arif returned from India, looking like he'd been starved to death. He couldn't find Kashmir and no matter how hard I pressed, he wouldn't talk about what had gone on.

As if that wasn't bad enough, Mum and Mick announced their engagement. That really knocked me for six. Mum made me so angry when she didn't want to see the photographs I'd taken of Dad's grave. She insisted all that was in the past and she wanted to look to the future.

Travelling back and forth to Leeds was a drag, so I teamed up with Moira, a girl from work, and moved in with her. Things were good for a while, but then disaster struck and all of a sudden leaving home didn't seem to be such a good idea any more. Mum, as usual, was right and I was too damn proud to admit I had my regrets. For ages now I've been dangling on a thin thread like a spider waiting for lunch to fly its way. What really annoys me is I had a good job and was making enough money to keep my head above water. But after today I guess I won't be getting paid again!

At the start, working at Rhodes and Co was enjoyable. I actually looked forward to getting up in the mornings. Life around the office became quite hectic when Cindy and Moira both set their sights on the same guy. Cindy made most of the trouble, she's such a tart! Masses of curls, flaming red lipstick and nails like claws. The woman looks like a bloody Barbie doll and she's not the easiest person in the world to get on with. She couldn't stand the sight of Moira and, to tell you the truth, Moira didn't exactly take to her either. There was a lot of static between them.

The three of us were thrown together because we worked in the same department. Rhodes and Co cater for children, they supply clothes, shoes and toys to the shops. My job involved taking telephone orders, making out invoices and informing the packers down in the warehouse what goods to send where. Moira did more or less the same thing, but also had to do a bit of the publicity work by drumming up new trade for the company.

In my opinion, Cindy had the best job. She got to sit around looking stunning, while Moira and I did all the real work.

The company has a shop at the back of the building and I liked working there. It was far better than sitting in the office having to observe Cindy's pouts and Moira's dark scowls.

Moira's a mad creature, but her heart's in the right place. She's got a slight weight problem and Cindy's always keen to point it out to her. This makes Moira very aggressive and a danger to live with because she's always breathing down my neck when I'm eating. Moira has her own faults. Take, for example, her taste in clothes. My God, I've never seen so many fluorescent colours in one place. She's also got this thing about earrings and finds it impossible to walk past a shop where they're sold without buying a pair. I'm willing to bet she'd wear bricks from her ears if they were in fashion.

Now let me dissect Cindy. With a figure like a fashion model and a voice that drips honey whenever she wants anything, the woman has the knack of worming herself out of any sort of tricky situation. Smug cow!

The day I arrived for work is vividly printed on my mind. Moira bounced over to me like a friendly puppy. 'Hi, I'm Moira Philips. It's good to meet you!' She shook my hand with such vigour, I honestly thought my arm was going to come loose.

The secretary sat at her desk and flicked an imaginary blonde curl over her shoulder. She gave me the once over. It was the kind of look that made me feel as though I had hairs sprouting out of my nostrils. Reaching elegantly for the phone, she spoke in a husky voice that even Marilyn Monroe would have killed for. 'Excuse me Mr Rhodes, I'm sorry to bother you, but the new girl has arrived.'

Mr Rhodes is a tall man in his early thirties, with thinning brown hair and a stern face, that seems to say 'No fun without me.' After giving me a welcome speech, he sent me on my way, with instructions to Moira who was to show me the ropes.

'You'll like it here,'she informed me as she taught me how to fill in an invoice. 'Just ask if you get stuck.'

'Who's she?'I asked pointing towards the secretary.

Moira pulled a sour face. 'Cindy Travers. She's a troublemaker. I'd stay out of her way if I were you. '

By lunchtime, I'd done some work. The canteen was full. Sitting alone I ate my fish and chips. Moira was in the office when I got back. She was reading a romance, a bag of toffees in front of her on the desk. 'Hi,' she said absently. 'Want one?'

'No, thanks. I've just eaten. Where's Miss World?'

'In the ladies room powdering her hooter.'

Rolling a sheet of paper into my typewriter, I sat down and stared at it. Cindy clicked past in her high heels. A cloud of perfume engulfed me.

'Haven't you got anything better to do than read that trash?' she asked, waspishly.

Chomping as loudly as she could, Moira ignored her.

'Manners of a pig!'Cindy muttered as she poured herself a coffee and unwrapped her Ryvitas. 'I bet you read every love story that comes out. I feel sorry for you Moira, you're such a loser.'

I stared at her in disbelief. What a bitch! Moira put down her book and gave Cindy a withering look. I could tell she was thinking of something to say. Come on, I urged silently, don't just sit there, fight back. I was disappointed when she didn't retaliate.

Cindy perched her behind on Moira's desk. I'd have pushed her off. Moira acted like she wasn't there.

'What's the matter fatty? Has the cat got your tongue?'

Slowly unwrapping another toffee, Moira popped it into her mouth. Cindy was out to get attention. Suddenly, she snatched the book out of Moira's hand and danced around the office with it.

'Give it back!'

'Or else?' Cindy dangled the book in front of Moira's face. 'You want it, you go and get it!' Then she hurled the book out of the window.

Moira rushed to her feet. 'One of these days you're going to get it.'

'Run along and fetch your book, Moira!'

She slammed out of the room. Cindy patted her curls at her desk and said, 'She's such a pain.'

I'd been travelling back and forth from Bradford to Leeds for a few weeks and decided it was time to stick in one place. I put this to Moira one afternoon as I made out an order for a consignment of night dresses.

'You could always move in with me,' she offered.

'Really?'

'Yeah, sure. I don't mind. I could do with the company.'

'How big is your place?'

'It's not bad, if you want you can come and have a look around. If you like it, we'll ask Mrs Rigsby, the landlady, to draw up a tenancy deal.'

Cindy came out of Mr Rhodes' office. 'What are you two whispering about? You look as thick as thieves.'

'Stacey's moving in with me,' Moira announced brightly.

Cindy said, 'What are you, Stacey? A glutton for punishment?'

'It's none of your business,' I bit back.

'I'd have thought you'd had enough of Moira in the office. Double helpings of her isn't good for the health!' Sitting down in her swivel chair, she crossed her legs.

Moira gave her a frosty glare. 'You think you're really smart. Well, you're not! What Stacey does is entirely her own business.'

They wanted to quarrel again. Rather reluctantly, I said, 'I'll see you two later. I've got to go down and see the order for these dresses goes through.'

They both ignored me as they sized each other up with looks of pure hatred.

Leaving Moira and Cindy alone wasn't the hottest thing to do. They were at each other's throats when I returned.

'If you think Gary would want to go out with you, then you're very much mistaken,' sneered Cindy. 'Face it Moira, you're not his type.'

'And a tart like you is?' Moira asked, her hands on her ample hips.

'I'll pretend I didn't hear that. You've got a nasty tongue Moira.'

'Aw, go to hell. One of these days someone's going to knock your teeth down your throat.'

Throwing back her head, Cindy laughed huskily. 'Just get on with your job.'

Scowling, Moira poured herself a coffee and picked up the 'phone. Cindy pulled a face at her and began to type.

Moira was slightly uncomfortable about taking me round to the flat. 'You might not like it Stacey. I made it all nice and clean for your arrival, but there are things you'll think are childish.'

'Don't worry, Moira, everything's going to be fine. I can't figure you out sometimes. What's the problem?'

'Nothing Stacey, just wait and see. There's a couple in the flat above, they keep pretty much to themselves. I've got the middle floor.'

The house was a terraced one in Rose Crescent. Moira unlocked the door and led me up the wide flight of stairs. She opened her door and we stepped inside. A hot flush spread across her face.

'Moira, this is beautiful!' I exclaimed.

'You're not just saying that are you?'

'It's fantastic.' I took a better look around. The living-room was decorated with forget-me-not wallpaper. Not my taste, but Moira's a bit of a weirdo, in the nicest possible way. I knocked the small macrame basket hanging from a hook under the window. Maybe I was feeling nervous, picking up on Moira's sense of insecurity. A small pill bottle rolled to the floor. Moira bent to pick it up.

'Let me introduce my companions,' she said abruptly. A wonderful array of fluffy toys took pride of place on the bright blue leather couch.

'This place is a zoo!' I grinned.

Moira smiled at me. 'Do you like it?'

I nodded and pointed to the smoked-glass table. 'That's a beauty. Where'd you get it?'

'My mum bought me it.'

Behind the door was a magazine rack and a bookshelf crammed full of romance novels. 'You've got your own library,' I commented as I sat down on the fluffy, white rug which had a seal cub reclining on it. Unlocking the window, Moira flopped down on the couch. 'My feet are killing me. Feel free to wander around. We'll be sharing the bedroom, I hope you don't mind.'

'That's fine,' I got to my feet and went to the bathroom. The bathroom suite was a pale green. A great big plastic frog was perched on the bath rack. Moira was very neat and tidy. The shelf over the toilet was stacked with toiletries and cleaning products. Moving on, I màde my way to the bedroom. There were two single beds and a stereo system in one corner of the room. An elegantly-carved dressing table and stool stood under the large window. Again, there was a book-stand full of romance stories. I picked one up and flicked through it. Then I went to find the kitchen which was next door to the bedroom. It was small, two people couldn't stand side by side in there. I was relieved to see Moira had a washing machine and fridge.

Moira asked me if I liked it.

'What was all the fuss about?'

She looked sheepish. 'I know you're not the mushy type. I was worried the toys and decor might put you off.'

'I love it. But there is a problem. I'm not as tidy as you, so don't lose your wig if the place starts looking messy.'

'I don't mind,'she said good-naturedly. 'Make yourself at home.'

That evening I stayed and did the cooking. Nothing fancy. Beans on toast. Moira didn't seem to enjoy it. I watched her quietly as she pushed the food around her plate. After a while, she began to get on my nerves. 'What's up with you?' I asked through a mouthful.

'I'm trying to lose weight and it's bloody hard work. I could kill Cindy with her bust in the right place and legs that go on forever. My body looks like it went for a walk and all the bits didn't quite make it back home. I hate myself.'

The girl was upset and I had to reassure her. Why did she envy Cindy?

'So you're saying I might as well stop fighting?'

'No! Don't twist it, Moira. You're a lovely person. Why do you want to be like Cindy?'

'Because she's beautiful and always has a good time,' she wailed.

'How do you know she has a good time?'

'I've been working with her for two years. All the guys swarm around her like bees around a bloody honey pot. In all that time, I've never had a date.'

'Well, neither have I! My boyfriend ditched me, and I haven't been out since. You and I should go out together.'

Moira shook her head and cleared the table. 'Not while I look like a sack of potatoes. I'm so self-conscious.'

'You're getting worked up about nothing!'

'Yeah, sure. Look at me. I weigh twelve stone and I look hideous. I'll be happy when I'm down to eight stone.'

There was no point in arguing with her. I let the subject drop and went to watch *Brookside*.

Moira was completely obsessed with her weight, all the magazines she owned had the diet tips and pages underlined.

At breakfast Moira sipped her orange juice slowly and tipped the remainder down the sink. I devoured two slices of toast and a bowl of sugar puffs and was ready to face the day. We walked to work. Then, as we went into the lobby, Moira told me she'd meet me upstairs. Getting into the lift, I checked my make-up and headed for the office. As I pushed open the door, I found Cindy going through Moira's drawer.

'What the hell are you doing?'

Cindy had been taken by surprise. 'Erm.... I'm looking for a rubber,' she lied.

I hung my jacket up and said, 'There's one on your desk. You've got no

106

right to go rummaging through her property.'

Cindy flashed me a smile. I noticed how quickly she regained her wits. 'I told you, Stacey, I was looking for a rubber.'

'Why don't I believe you? Just leave Moira alone.'

'Don't tell me what to do. That fat bun deserves everything she gets. Oh, by the way, Morris told me to let you know you'll be working in the shop today.'

Exercising great self control, I checked my in-tray for work to be completed.

Morris walked out of the adjoining office. 'Ah, Stacey, has Cindy told you that I want you down in the shop?'

'Yes, Mr Rhodes.'

'When Moira decides to put in an appearance, ask her to help you.'

Cindy turned on the charm. 'What about me? What shall I do?'

Morris slapped her behind. 'You stay here and look beautiful Cindy.' Then he turned and went into his office and closed the door.

Moira rushed in and took off her coat. 'You're late!' Cindy informed her.

'Big deal! What's it to you?'

Cindy bristled. 'You should make the effort to get here on time.'

'Shut your gob.' Moira sat down and checked her diary.

'You're always slowing us down,' Cindy shot back as she stapled a pile of papers together.

Chewing the inside of her cheek, Moira asked Cindy what her problem was.

'You're the problem. We need people who are efficient and willing to work.'

Moira looked very smug. 'If you must know, Cindy, I went to see Gary.'

Cindy paled before our very eyes. 'Keep your hands off Gary, he's mine.' The tigress had her claws out.

Moira grinned. 'So was Mark from Computers and so was Joe from the canteen and let's not forget Tony from the depot. What do you do with 'em all? You go through men like I do toffees. You don't scare me, Cindy. I'll do what I like when I like.'

For once Cindy seemed to have an attack of lock-jaw. Moira had surprised me with her outburst. It was heartening to see she wasn't going to take Cindy's bullying lying down.

Moira set about her work briskly. Cindy watched her with a bewildered look on her pretty face. I bet she was finding it difficult to believe Moira had actually been to see Gary.

'Come on, Moira, we've got to go down to the shop.'

She got to her feet. 'Do I have to? I've got stacks of work to get through. I hate working in that bloody place.'

Pulling herself up straight, Cindy spoke. 'Morris said you've got to help out so get going!'

'Mind your own business, Cindy. I was talking to Stacey. You're just jealous because I managed to get a date with Gary.'

Cindy spluttered in disbelief. 'He'll drop you like a hot potato, Moira. It's me he wants.'

'Yeah sure, that's why he's taking me out tonight! Wake up and smell the flowers.' Moira seemed to be enjoying herself until Cindy said, 'You're a fool, Moira. Yesterday when I went up to the computer department I happened to hear Matt and Gary talking about you. Matt said you had no dress sense and Gary said you looked a right mess. '

I pushed Moira towards the door and told her to take no notice. Cindy knew she'd hit the target and said, 'And they have got a point. You really do need help with your wardrobe.'

Marching over to Cindy's desk, Moira picked up a neat pile of paper work and scattered it all over the crimson carpet. Cindy screamed and ordered Moira to pick up the mess. Moira shook her head. There was no way Cindy was prepared to lose face. 'You pick them up,' she said to me.

'On yer bike!' I said rudely as I opened the door.

Cindy got to her feet and straightened her skirt, which looked more like a headband. 'I'm going to tell Morris,' she exclaimed.

She was saved the trouble. The man himself came out. 'What's going on here?' he demanded as he observed the loose leaf paper all over the place. We didn't reply. He tapped his brogue shoe impatiently. I wanted to stomp on it.

Cindy was quite an actress. Burying her face in her hands, she started crying. Morris told her to go and wash her face. As I bent to pick up the mess, Morris said he wanted to see us in his office.

'I'll get that bitch,' muttered Moira. 'I swear I will!'

'Give it a rest, Moira. We're in enough trouble as it is. 'I made a scraggy-looking pile and went to knock on Morris's door.

'Come in.' The biggest slime-ball in Leeds spoke. He had his back to us and didn't turn round straightaway. He continued to gaze out of the window. It's annoying when people do that. It gives them an air of false superiority. A great big desk and a black leather chair were in the middle of the office. My feet sank into the shaggy pile carpet. There were filing cabinets placed neatly against one wall, a chaise-longue under the window. The place must have cost an arm and a leg to furnish. Most probably his dad's.

When he ordered us to sit down, I was reminded of school days . Any minute now and he'd give us a detention. Then he came up behind me, placed his hands on my shoulders and squeezed. Revulsion coursed through my body. He asked me if I was happy working for him. I bit my lips and could still feel the pressure of his hands even when he'd moved off. He told Moira she wasn't pulling her weight. That was ironic, she was trying too lose the damn stuff, not put it on.

Moira almost died when he told her she had to put in some overtime. He wanted her to stay behind after work. She couldn't miss her date, not even for Morris and his crummy job. She said she had a dental appointment. Morris pointed out she'd have to cancel. Moira refused politely telling him her tooth needed filling. I don't know why but I did it. I went and volunteered to stay on for her.

Looking me up and down, Morris said to Moira, 'You can go, I don't want any trouble from you. Let's keep it nice and friendly.'

My stomach churned, I was beginning to regret being so hasty. Morris sat down and said, 'There will be a lot of work for you to get through. I hope you're prepared for it.'

That evening, I had to put up with Morris and his advances for almost two hours. He was like a bloody octopus. If he wasn't accidentally bumping into me, he was leaning over me to correct typing mistakes. I wanted to scream. I finished one lot of invoices and orders, then Morris gave me a stack of letters which had to be mailed. That was Cindy's job. I slogged through them as fast as I could, then got to my feet.

'Have you completed them?'

'Yes, it's all done. Is there anything else?'

'Relax Stacey, I'll give you a lift home.'

The thought of being cooped up in a car with Morris was too much. 'No, there's no need. I can walk.'

'Call me Morris,' he insisted, 'I want to be your friend.'

I would have enjoyed throttling him. He handed me a folder and pointed out some company names. 'This is normally Moira's job, but you might as well get to grips with it. You never know when a promotion might come up,' he winked slyly.

Just what the hell was he hinting at? It sounded like a classic case of you scratch my back and I'll happily scratch yours.

'Be a good girl and call these people. Tell them it will be to their advantage if they give us the contract for winter wear.'

I took the file from him. My hand shook slightly as I dialled the number. The 'phone rang several times before I replaced the receiver.

'Nothing,' I informed him. 'I'd better get going.'

'Why don't you let me buy you a drink?'

'I don't drink.' I said truthfully. Making a quick getaway, I cursed Moira for leaving me to do her dirty work. When I arrived home, there was no sign of Moira. She'd left a note on the fridge door. 'Stacey, thanks for helping me out. I really appreciate it. I've ordered pizza for you. It'll be there at 8.30. Love Moira.'

Moira had been seeing Gary for a month. He was a tall, slim guy with blonde hair and blue eyes. Moira was happy and when she was happy, I never got a word in any way at all. For hours she'd rave on about what Gary did and what Gary said. She was making me feel like an old maid. If Moira could get herself a man and make a go of things, why couldn't I?

It was the middle of November. Moira was on another diet, she was losing weight and looked good. I decided it was time to go and see Mum for the weekend. Moira was off to see Gary's parents. It looked like they were serious about each other. As I packed an overnight bag Moira told me she was getting engaged to Gary. I was happy for her. She was grinning from ear to ear and told me she never thought anything as good as Gary would ever come her way.

She made me promise I wouldn't mention her engagement to Cindy who was still trying to get her claws into Gary. 'You'll have to be my bridesmaid Stacey, what do you say?'

'Okay, as long as I get to choose my own dress.'

I was in for a big surprise when I got home. Mum greeted me with her usual smile and hug. She looked so happy. Her hair had been cut and curled and she wore a beaded blouse and cream slacks.

As I made myself a cup of tea, she broke it to me there was something she had to say. Mick had asked her to marry him and she'd accepted. I almost dropped the cup. She was winding me up for sure.

'Stacey, love, I want you to be happy for me. Will you be my chief bridesmaid?'

'You're the second person who's asked me that today. I'd love to be your bridesmaid. When's the big day?'

'We've decided to get married on January tenth. Naveed's going to give me away.'

'How did he take the news?'

'He's happy for me. To tell you the truth, I'm relieved you didn't give me a hard time. I'm going to get married in style. I want everything to be perfect. My dress is a pale cream and it's lovely.'

'What's mine like?'

'Emerald green. You can decide on the design. I've seen the sort of dress I'd like you to wear in the catalogues. Let's go into the living room and I'll show you.'

The dress she'd selected had a low scoop neck, with a bow at the front which gathered up to form sleeves. It had a dropped waist and flared skirt. 'You'll wear white shoes and a fresh flower headband. What do you think?'

There wasn't much to think. I was shocked but there was no way I was going to let on. She showed me the dress she'd picked for herself. It was ankle length, handkerchief style and all lace.

'There's a headband with it, and I've got some white shoes as well. Stacey, be honest with me. If you don't like your dress, you can always have some of the details changed. The dressmaker's in Baildon.'

I assured her everything was perfect and said I wanted to go and see Aunt Razia.

Aunt Razia was in better spirits, she told me that Sammy was expecting again. Uncle Naveed had promised to let her come back home if Umar didn't get his visa in December.

She filled me in on all the local gossip. Arif was on speaking terms with his dad again and he was working in the shop full-time. After finishing my tea I headed home. Outside the air was chilly. A thick fog had crept up suddenly and I shivered as the cold nipped my nose and fingers. The night air smelt frosty. Mick and Mum were in the livingroom. Congratulating him on snaring my Mum, I went up to bed. Behind closed doors I gave into my real feelings. All afternoon, I'd painted a false smile on my dial and pretended everything was brilliant, when all the time Mum's news had hit me like a thunderbolt.

Dad's photo smiled at me from the bedside table. How could Mum be so inconsiderate? Fancy picking the same wedding date twice! When Dad had given us everything. She had no right to settle for second best! That's what Mick was! I know I was being totally selfish, I couldn't help it. Mum had changed so much, she'd more confidence and knew what she wanted out of life, whereas I felt like a total failure. Crying into my pillow, I fell asleep.

I spent Sunday in a state of stupefied pretence. The effort of keeping smiling was killing me. Mick offered to drive me back to Leeds and then tried to talk to me. 'It's good news about your mum and me, don't you think?' He scratched his ginger beard noisily.

'It's okay. Don't expect me to call you Dad, I'm too old for all that!'

He waited for the lights to change and drove on. 'I don't expect anything of the sort. I want to be your friend.'

He was so bloody boring. 'Your mum's going to pack in her job and, after our honeymoon we'll be moving to Scotland.'

My mouth hit the ground. 'Scotland!' I squeaked.

Mick nodded as the car came to stop at the zebra crossing. 'I've got work there and your mum could do with a change.'

Talk about mad! Mum hadn't told me about her intentions. Maybe she was afraid I'd chuck a tantrum.

'You can drop me here.' I pointed to the road at the bottom of Rose Crescent.

'Stacey, do you need money?' He was trying to be kind.

'I've got a job, remember!' I slammed the door and walked away. There was no-one in the street and no cars passed. It was as though I was the only human being around. I felt wretched. Life had given me nothing but disappointments. I was so angry and jealous! I had my own flat, a job that paid good money and yet I still begrudged Mum her happiness.

A feeling of deep pain crept over me as I let myself into the flat. Moira hadn't got back from Gary's.

The room was quiet. I kicked off my shoes, switched on the telly and padded into the kitchen. I plugged in the kettle and waited for it to boil. I needed to talk to somebody who would understand how I felt. I found myself longing for Sammy's company. 'Damn this!' I cursed bitterly. 'Damn, damn, damn, and to hell with Mick, the bloody ginger nut!'

Mum would have had plenty to say if she could've heard me. At least I didn't have to live with them.

A very cheerful Moira returned home that night. 'I've got so much to tell you,' she gushed enthusiastically as she unpacked her case. 'Gary's mum and dad are great, he's got two brothers and a sister. His mum's invited me to stay again next week and....'

'Slow down for God's sake!' I snapped not giving her a chance to finish.

'What's wrong, Stacey?'

'Nothing. Just take it easy.'

Moira shook her head. 'Forget it. It's obvious you're not interested. I'm going to have a bath.'

Get lost, I wanted to add, but managed to say, 'Moira, come on. I didn't mean to jump down your throat.'

She sat down and looked at me. 'What's wrong, Stacey? You look like an accident waiting to happen.'

'I really appreciate the compliment.'

'Stacey!'

'Mum's getting married.'

Moira's squeal of delight almost ruptured my ear drums. 'That's fantastic, when's the wedding?'

'Who cares?' I sulked.

Moira smiled at me. I was sick to death of everybody smiling at me. Did they think I didn't know how to?

'Do you want to talk about it?' She balanced a soft toy on her head.

An involuntary laugh escaped. 'I'm pissed off, that's all.'

Moira turned out to be quite a good listener. She nodded now and then. Talking to her helped me to understand the turmoil of my feelings.

'Stop brooding, Stacey, it won't help. Your mum needs your support. If she realises you're not keen to stand by her, then you'll lose her for good.' She scratched her nose and continued. 'It's not as if Scotland's on the moon. You can always visit her and your step-dad.'

'Thanks Moira, I really needed a shoulder to cry on.'

'That's okay, these shoulders are big enough for the whole of Leeds to cry on.'

I hugged her. 'Hell, we've got work in the morning. Piss-head Morris and tarty Cindy here we come!'

I couldn't help grinning. She made me feel tons better.

A week later disaster struck. Gary let slip that Cindy had invited him to her flat for a drink. Moira was as mad as a bull in a china shop. 'I'll kill her,' she threatened. 'Honest to God I will! How dare she invite my fiance round for a drink? Gary had no right to accept.' She stormed around the place with a duster.

'Watch out, Moira, you'll break something.'

'I know what I'd like to break,' she seethed. 'Cindy's neck. How dare she?'

'I don't know. Come on. Leave the dusting, we'll be late for work.'

'You go ahead, I'll catch you up.'

Not wanting to run into Morris for being late, I dashed through the pouring rain. By the time I got to the office water dripped from my limp hair. Cindy stood by the filing cabinet, a file in her hand.

'Hello Stacey,' she muttered, 'where's your fatter half?'

'That's not funny.' I hung my coat up. 'What's been going on with you and Gary?'

'Wouldn't you like to know?' Leaning against the table she ran her taloned fingers through her hair. 'Gary's not Moira's type.'

'Who is then?'

'The marshmallow man from *Ghostbusters*,' she sniggered.

'You'd better watch yourself Cindy. Moira's out to get you.'

Cindy dismissed my warning with the wave of her hand. 'Moira can't hurt me. Gary's my sort of guy and I intend to keep him.'

'He's engaged to Moira.' I remarked as I tore open a packet of blu-tac.

'Engagements can be broken.'

'You're a bitch.'

'I know,' she laughed. 'I can't wait to see the look on Moira's face when she finds out.'

'She already knows.'

'Who told her?'

'Gary did!'

Morris spoke on the intercom system. 'Cindy, I'd like you to come and take some dictation please.'

'I'll be with you in a minute, Mr Rhodes.' Sighing lightly, she sharpened her green pencil and picked up her note pad. 'Tell Moira I said Gary's a terrific lay.'

I tried to concentrate on the invoice in front of me. Everybody knew that Cindy had a reputation as long as her legs. Had Gary really gone to bed with her? Moira would rip his head off if it was true.

Moira decided it was time to put in an appearance, she was chewing a huge wad of gum.

'Where's the tart?'

'Moira, don't let her provoke you, she's in there with face-ache.'

'I bet she's washing his tonsils for him.' She lingered for a while near Cindy's desk and then went to sit down. Cindy opened the door and teetered out.

'There's a bad smell in here,' Moira said.

'Take a wash then,' Cindy retorted.

'You bitch!'

'Have you got something to say to me, Moira?'

Moira's face flushed angrily. 'You keep your hands off Gary, or else you'll get a good belting.'

Cindy sat down and glared at Moira. 'Are you threatening me?'

'Yes!'

'I'm going to tell Morris.' Cindy got to her feet. A long string of chewing gum stretched upwards with her. I tried not to laugh.

'Where did that come from?' Cindy shrieked.

Moira shrugged her shoulders. 'Don't ask us.'

'You vicious cow!' She plucked the gooey mess from her skirt. 'It's ruined because of you.'

'I didn't do anything,' Moira said.

Cindy stamped her foot childishly. 'I'm going to tell Morris.'

Moira laughed.'Go on. See if I care.'

'You ruined my brand-new skirt.'

'Pardon me,' Moira raised her eyebrows. 'Is that what it is? Sorry I thought it was a tea towel.'

'Shut your mouth, Porky pig!'

Dear Moira, she really made my day. She did the unthinkable. I watched in stunned silence as she threw the contents of her cup in Cindy's face. The way she howled anyone would've thought she was being murdered.

Morris, disturbed by the racket, came out to investigate.

'What the hell is going on?'

Cindy wailed. 'Mr Rhodes, look what Moira's done.' She pointed at the rear end of her skirt.

The 'phone rang, I answered it while Morris ushered Moira and Cindy into his office. I wanted to listen at the door but the damn 'phone call made me miss all the action. A consignment of winter wear had been sent to the wrong store by mistake. I had to go down to the warehouse and sort out the paper work. I passed Gary in the hall. He smiled at me, I didn't return the gesture.

The depot was busy. The vans parked outside were loading up with supplies. It took me ages to find Peter, the guy in charge of deliveries. He informed me that a lorry-load of clothes had been sent out to a shop in Harrogate. The owners of the shop had refused the order. They claimed they hadn't ordered anything from us. It took a while to explain to Peter I made the deal with the clothing company, Andreas, and they'd signed a contract. If he had a problem, then he should contact us. Finally, I went back upstairs.

The sound of muffled crying sent me running into the cloakroom where Moira sat with her face covered. 'Moira, what happened?'

'I can't go on like this,' she sobbed. 'I can't compete with her.'

'Do you want a glass of water?'

She shook her head. 'She said some awful things to me.'

I could well imagine what she'd said. Cindy needed a good smack.

'What am I going to do? Gary went to bed with her.'

'You don't know she's telling the truth.' I wanted to reassure her. Cindy was the sort of person who would actually stoop so low and steal somebody else's boyfriend. It was in her nature! 'Have you spoken to Gary?'

'I can't face him.'

'Where's Cindy?'

'She went home to get the till receipt for her skirt. Morris said I've got to pay for the damage. I was saving up for the wedding.'

Her face was puffed and her eyes were red-rimmed and swollen. 'I wish I was dead!'

'Stop it, Moira. Come on, let's go and get something to eat.'

Cindy had changed her clothes. She was wearing a red skirt and blouse and looked the part of the scarlet woman. After washing her face and pulling a comb through her hair, Moira came out of the cloakroom and sat down at her desk.

Cindy watched her. I was under the impression she'd keep her trap shut. Hell would freeze over before she ever did that. Sucking the end of her pencil, she remarked on Moira's appearance. 'Looks like something the cat dragged in.'

Glaring at her, I said, 'Pack it in Cindy!'

'Well it's true. Look at her. She's such a loser. Hey Moira, that mole on Gary's hip is really cute, don't you think?'

Moira froze, she looked ready to flake out.

'I told him it looks sexy,' she stated.

'I hate you Cindy,' then Moira dashed out of the office.

When she didn't turn up after lunch, I began to worry. Cindy had pushed her to the edge enjoying every moment of Moira's discomfort.

I'm quite free with my fists, but that day I sat like a lump on a log and listened to Cindy prattling on about Moira. Not about to voice my concern in front of Cindy, I 'phoned the flat to see if Moira had gone there. No reply. She'd most probably gone for a walk and lost all track of time.

At five-thirty, I got ready to go home. I covered the electric typewriter and pushed back my chair.

'Stacey, will you stay behind and do some overtime?' Morris asked.

He had to be joking! I had no desire to repeat an exercise in sexual harrassment again. 'I'm sorry, I can't.'

'I never got to thank you for helping me get the Andreas account. Let me take you out for a drink.'

'It's all part of the job, sir. Moira does it all the time.'

He ran his fat fingers through his thinning hair and smiled. 'Well, you're not Moira. Come on Stacey, I could do with a hand.'

'I'm busy tonight,' I informed him, eager to get home.

'Well, I want you to stay.'

He was trying to force me against my will. I couldn't tolerate his roaming hands and arrogance. The pervert, trying to touch me up all the time. I felt sick!

'You can't make me stay, Mr Rhodes. I've got to go now!'

'I'm your boss Stacey. Don't you think it would be in your interest to stay and help me out?'

'Maybe some other time.' I grabbed my coat and headed for the door. Morris blocked the way. 'You've got a very big chip on your shoulder. I'd say about the size of the Rock of Gibraltar,' he informed me.

And I'd love to drop it on your head, you swine! I told myself. It was a rotten stunt to pull, him trying to force himself on me. He enjoyed coming up behind me and watching me work. I hated that, my fingers would hit all the wrong keys and my concentration would be shot to pieces.

The 'phone in his office rang. Talk about being saved by the bell! 'Don't go away,' he winked as he left. The guy had rocks in his head. Did he honestly expect me to wait around for him. I ran for my life! One day Morris was going to go too far and end up in deep shit!

In Rose Crescent, the front door was open. My heart sank. I thought we'd been burgled. Stepping cautiously inside, I scanned the situation. There appeared to be no sign of disturbance. Everything seemed to be in place. Locking the door behind me, I tip-toed into the living room. Moira's handbag lay on the floor, its contents scattered all over the carpet. I tossed my coat on the couch, scooped up her stuff and went to find her.

The curtains in the bedroom had been drawn. I switched on the light and called out to Moira. She didn't reply. She was lying on the bed with her mouth open. A small bottle of pills by her side.

'Moira, Moira wake up.'

Her skin felt clammy to the touch. I took her by the arms and tried to raise her. I gasped when her head flopped to one side. She was unconscious.

Panic gripped me first of all, making it impossible for me to think straight. I tried to remember what to do in this sort of a situation. Breathing slowly to calm myself, I went into the living room and called for an ambulance.

Back in the bedroom I sat with Moira and waited. Her breathing was shallow. A few moments later, a siren sounded. Relief made me sag. I ran downstairs to open the door. The ambulance-men were good at their job. I was quite convinced Moira was dead and stood back watching through a blur of tears. They wheeled her out of the flat on a stretcher.

At the hospital, they wouldn't allow me into the cubicle as they set to work due to the fact I wasn't related to Moira. Sitting in the waiting room, I prayed she'd pull through and promised myself I'd kill her once she made it out alive!

After what seemed like hours, a doctor came out to see me. 'How is she?' I was close to tears.

'It was touch and go for a while, but we've managed to save her. We're taking her into the ward now.'

'Can I see her?'

He shook his head and told me Moira needed to rest. If I wanted, I could come back in the morning. He expected me to go home as though nothing had happened. I tried to reason with him but he sent me packing.

I went to the flat, my mind a hive of activity. I had to let Moira's parents know. Rummaging through Moira's handbag I found her 'phone book and called them up. The only other person to contact was Gary. I didn't know if he'd be interested and wavered as I picked up the 'phone. What the hell! I'd make sure he didn't get a decent night's sleep.

His 'phone rang three times before he answered it. 'Hello.'

'Is that you Gary? This is Stacey.'

He yawned loudly. 'Yeah, what's up?'

'I thought you might like to know your fiancee took an overdose and she's in hospital.'

'Which hospital?'

'Find out! I thought that you were a good guy, looks like I was wrong!' Then I slammed the 'phone down, and sat for a while.

The moment I awoke the next morning, all the events of the previous day came rushing back. Skipping breakfast, I called the hospital. They refused to give out any information on the 'phone. After a quick shower, I got ready for work. Dressed in a black pair of jeans and a long blue shirt, I applied a light coat of lipgloss and eye pencil. My hair was getting out of hand, it needed trimming. Tying it back in a pony tail, I left the flat. The miserable weather didn't help to pull me out of the doldrums. It was cold, windy and wet.

The office was warm and quiet. The ringing 'phone shattered the silence occasionally. My mind was a blank. I knew I wasn't in any state to work. Cindy came out of the cloakroom. 'You look awful,' she announced as she patted her curls and sat down. 'I bet you had a wild night.What did you get up to?'

Her prattling made my hackles rise. 'If you must know, you little bitch, I spent most of it in hospital.'

Her eyebrows rose in surprise. 'Why are you swearing at me?'

I went off at the deep end. 'Because it's your fault! You wouldn't lay off Moira. She took an overdose and almost died!'

Cindy's blushered face turned a ghastly pale. Clapping a hand over her mouth, she closed her eyes. 'You're to blame, Cindy. You wouldn't leave her alone. Out of all the guys to go for, you had to take the one she loves.'

Cindy's lower lip trembled.

Rushing towards her I said, 'Don't you dare turn on the water works. When I've finished with you, you'll wish you'd never set eyes on Gary!'

'Stacey, it was only a joke. Nothing happened!'

'My God!' I exploded, 'Of all the rotten things to do. I'm warning you, Cindy, if you're lying to me you've had it!'

'Ask Gary if you don't believe me,' she wailed. 'I swear to you Stacey, nothing happened.'

'You try telling that to Moira,' I screamed in frustration.

Cindy cowered in her chair. 'Stacey you've got to believe me.'

'What is going on?'

Reeling around, I saw Morris standing in the doorway.

'Ask her,' I yelled, 'She drove Moira to the edge and helped to push her off. She tried to kill herself.'

'Calm down, Stacey,you're getting carried away. What happened?'

I was getting carried away! The nerve of the man. Didn't anybody care about Moira? 'You ask her, she'll tell you what happened.'

Morris frowned. 'Cindy what have you got to say for yourself?'

She had a lot to say. Bursting into tears said it all.

'You make me sick!' I fumed before storming off.

The clock in the corridor ticked away. My stomach felt as though it had been tied into knots. Rubbing my damp palms down my coat, I waited for the nurse. The flowers I bought lay on the bench by my side.

Moira's parents were with her. Gary sat facing me. I couldn't talk to him. He looked haggard, his hair needed combing and his clothes were wrinkled. Well, it bloody served him right! Sneaking a sly look at him every time his attention was distracted, I noticed the shadows under his eyes, and the frantic way his eyes darted all over the place.

'Miss Malik, you can go through now,' said the nurse. 'It's the cubicle right at the end, please leave the curtains closed.'

I let my feet lead me. Moira lay with her eyes closed, a drip attached to her left arm. Approaching the bed, I whispered her name softly. Her eyes flickered open, she was so pale.

A huge tear ran down her cheek. I pulled up a chair and looked at her. When she spoke, her voice sounded terrible. She apologised for scaring me and told me she had no desire to see Gary again. Cindy was free to take him. Moira didn't strike me as a loser. She'd always stood up to Cindy. There was no way she could give her the satisfaction of gloating. I told her so, but she didn't want to know. Her silence told me she wanted to be left alone. I promised to visit her again and left quietly.

Moira got better as you might expect, and Gary made Cindy tell the truth about what had really happened in her flat. Moira wanted to know about the mole on the hip revelation. Gary flushed and said that Cindy had spilt wine on his pants and he'd taken them off to wash out the stain. Cindy had walked in on him while he was in the bathroom.

After that, Gary became a fixture in our flat, never leaving Moira's side.

121

She enjoyed all the attention and began to get back to normal.

A week before Christmas '92, I did all my shopping and returned to Bradford. Mum wanted me to stay for Christmas. Promising to return on Christmas Eve, I told her I didn't want to miss the office party. Arif came to visit and the tight-fisted devil bought me a present. I wanted to open it straightaway but he wouldn't allow that. 'Open it on Christmas day. It's not much, but you'll like it.'

'Can you come and pick me up from Leeds on Christmas Eve?'

'Yeah, I'll borrow the van. And if you behave yourself, I might take you out to dinner.'

That sounded like a date. He certainly looked good in his white polo shirt and grey slacks.

I went to see Aunt Razia. Uncle Naveed let me in. On the way to the living room, I told him Mum wanted him to take us to Baildon for a dress fitting.

Aunt Razia was sitting in the armchair knitting a sweater for Sammy's baby. Seating myself on the floor by her feet, I enjoyed the heat of the fire. She told me that Sammy was coming home on the twenty-eighth. Uncle Naveed was upset Umar hadn't obtained his visa.

We both agreed it was great he'd have to stay in Pakistan and miss being there when the baby came along. I dragged myself up from the fire and told Aunt Razia I had to get off to Baildon. She nodded, put down her knitting needles and walked with me to the door, where she gave me a big hug. 'Come back soon, Stacey. I enjoy our chats.'

On the way to Baildon, Uncle Naveed asked a lot of questions. 'When are you going to give up this job Stacey?'

'Not yet!'

'I wish you would settle down. It's not right a pretty girl like you all on your own.'

Trying not to laugh, I said, 'Don't worry, Uncle. I'll survive.'

Sighing heavily, he muttered something I didn't quite catch. Mum winked at me. I knew Uncle Naveed felt he was no longer an important figure in my life. I didn't go running to him anymore. Not wishing to upset him I said, 'Uncle Naveed, when I do decide to get married, will you give me away?'

'I'll throw you at the poor man!' He roared with laughter.

The dress was perfect. I really liked it. As we left the dressmaker's, Mum said, 'Promise you'll be home on Christmas Eve, Stacey. I want Mick to feel part of the family.'

'Don't panic. I wouldn't miss it for the world.'

Moira and Gary had decorated our flat, it looked good. Paper chains and tinsel hung from the walls. The windows had been painted with imitation snow, and all the lights on the tree worked. On top of all that our flat smelt like a bakery. Moira wasn't going home to her parents, she'd invited them round to dinner. She baked and planned like an old hen. Gary helped her, looking as proud as punch.

Moira had Gary to accompany her to the party. I was on my own. If I'd taken the time out to ask Arif, he wouldn't have refused. But there was only so much of that guy I could stand.

My party-dress cost me a week's pay packet. It was made of soft, black velvet and the bodice and sleeves were embroidered with tiny pearls and sequins. I'd bought a pair of flat open-toed sandals and scrounged a purse from Moira. I hadn't been out for a while - it took me ages to get ready.

Moira was finished in less than ten minutes. She'd brushed her hair until it shone and her face looked beautiful.

To tell the truth, I'd never noticed how pretty Moira was. Her eyes looked massive, mascaraed and lined with pencil. Her cheeks glowed and her thin lips were painted a light pink colour. The blue party dress she wore made her eyes look darker than usual.

'Come on, Stacey. We'll be late.'

'Now look what you've made me do, ' I grumbled as my lip liner slipped.

'The taxi's here. Hurry up.' Thrusting my coat into my hands, she pushed me towards the door. 'We'll miss all the fun because of you.'

The whole of Rhodes and Company were to be present. The large conference room had been decorated, music blared loudly and people were dancing.

Morris was up to his old tricks, groping anything in a skirt. As soon as he spotted me, he came over. Staggering slightly, he put a glass into my hand. 'Here, drink this,' he breathed alcoholic fumes all over me. 'You look very sexy tonight,' he squeezed my behind.

'Cut that out!'

'What's the matter? You're such a sour puss. Be nice to me, it's Christmas.'

I tried to push my way through the dancing couples. Morris seized me by the arm. 'Dance with me.' He pressed himself against my body and nuzzled my neck.

'I don't want to.'

'Stop playing hard to get, Stacey,' he was clinging to me. I was positive I'd puke as my heart skidded across my insides.

The music pounded inside my head and those around me appeared to be twice their normal size. The glass fell from my hand and shattered.

I insisted I didn't want to dance. Morris refused to take no for an answer. His hold tightened so I couldn't breathe. Then, without any warning, his mouth swooped down to meet mine. Revulsion rose inside me. 'Get off me,' I yelled as I wiped my mouth with the back of my hand.

'Calm down, you silly girl. I only want to dance.'

I panicked. Reaching out, I clawed his face. 'Why, you hell cat!' he growled, lunging for me. Side-stepping quickly I watched him stumble in a drunken stupor. Seizing the opportunity for escape, I bumped into several dancers on my way out. A rough hand caught me and slammed me against the wall. The breath was knocked out of my body.

'You'll regret this,' hissed Morris as he clamped a hand over my mouth. I bit him so hard, his yelp of outrage scared me.

My legs shook. 'I'm going to report you.'

He sneered in my face. 'I haven't done anything wrong.'

'I've got witnesses. Don't think you'll get away with attacking me.'

'Come morning, those people will be too sozzled to remember anything. Nobody's going to believe you.'

'You touch me again and I'll scream. I've had it with you and this place. I'm quitting.'

Determined to have the last word, he said, 'You can't quit. You're fired!'

I ran down the corridor and out into the dark night.

It was snowing heavily, the biting cold chilled me to the bone. My body felt like elastic. I trudged through the snow and was shaking with fury. The more I thought about what had happened, the angrier I got. By the time I reached the flat I was so cold, I could hardly stand up straight. My hair was caked with snow and my dress was soaked.

To my horror, I realised I didn't have the key. In my haste to get away, I'd left my purse and coat behind! With numb fingers, I rang the bell praying that the couple above would hear me. They were out! The only other person with a key was the landlady. She lived two streets away. My nose was running and I couldn't stop shivering as I made my way to her house.

Trying to ring the bell was a waste of time. My hands were stiff with cold. Sinking down on the step I cried out.

A light shone in the hall and then, to my relief, the front door opened. Mrs Rigsby stood in the door. 'Stacey, is that you? Oh my God! What happened?'

I shook my head. She called her husband.He wasted no time in carrying me into the house. I felt faint and closed my eyes to stop the darting lights. Mrs Rigsby fussed around me. Trying to put a brave face on everything was hopeless. It crumpled along with my pride and I sobbed. Mrs Rigsby helped me out of my wet clothes. Bending down, she pulled off my shoes which made an unhappy squelching sound. Mr Rigsby called for the doctor while his wife towelled my hair. My head was aching. Mrs Rigsby gave me a glass of hot milk, something I hate. 'Here love, this'll help warm you up. Shall I call your mum?'

'No,' I said faintly. 'Don't do that, I'll be fine.'As I stood, the room whizzed round so fast I gasped. My ears pounded almost as though the sea was crashing around inside them. Lurching forward I fell and the flowered carpet rushed to meet me.

It was morning when I opened my eyes. God, how my head ached! The sound of voices and the rattle of cups and saucers alerted me to the fact I wasn't alone. As my eyes began to focus again, I noticed somebody standing by the window. I groaned as the pain cut through my body, I tried to sit up.

'Welcome back to the land of the living.'

Tears pricked my eyes at the sound of such a familiar voice.

'My, my I never thought I'd live to see the day you'd cry.'

'Arif, what happened?'

He came towards the bed and sat down. 'You stupid fool! You've had us all so worried. For a while back there I thought you were a goner.'

'I've got a whopper of a headache.'

'Do you remember what happened?'

'I can recall the party and then going to Mrs Rigsby's.'

'We all know you're nuts. I thought you wouldn't be stupid enough to go running around in the middle of the night in that excuse you call a dress.'

Frowning, I hoped to find a glimmer of humour in his eyes. There was none.

'Arif, don't. I feel awful.'

'Stacey, come back to Bradford with us.'

'Who's us?'

'Aunt Carla and myself.'

'Mum's here?'

'Yeah, sure she is. She wanted to take you back home last week when you flaked out.'

'Arif...what do you mean? It was last night.'

He shook his head. 'You've been ill for over a week. Ask your mum if you don't believe me.'

Mum nodded. I found it difficult to believe I'd lost a week from my life without even knowing about it. The thought scared me a bit.

'You said some wild stuff when you were delirious, 'Mum told me as she gave me a hug. 'I didn't know you called Mick a ginger nut.'

'Oh Mum, did I let it slip?' I was shocked.

'Yes and some other juicy scraps as well. Don't look so down. Make a speedy recovery for my wedding.'

I cringed. I might have said all sorts of things and I'd never get to find out about them. Me and my big mouth. Even when I was off the planet, I couldn't keep it shut.

Arif handed me the present he'd bought me. Inside the small box was a crystal cat wearing boxing gloves. 'That's you. Free with your fists and mouth.' He laughed and ruffled my hair.

So back to my appointment with Rhodes and Co. There were a few things to sort out before I actually left. During my illness, Arif had become far too protective. Moira had taken quite a shine to him. He could charm the birds out of the trees when he wanted to.

Pulling on my coat one morning, I told Arif I was going shopping. He offered to go for me. I didn't want him to find out where I was going, so I said, 'I've got a few personal purchases to make.'

The guy fussed like a mad thing all day long. Mum had left to make those last-minute arrangements before the wedding. Arif had promised to deliver me to the door for the big occasion.

Walking firmly out of the flat, I took the same route to work I'd taken for a year. When I got to the office, Cindy didn't speak to me. Morris was out on business and Moira was in the bog. Mr Rhodes senior had agreed to see me. His secretary made me sit in the waiting room for over an hour, the cheeky rat-bag.

Telling him my side of the story, I tried not to stare too much at his shiny bald head and gigantic grey moustache. Only when I'd finished, did he say that Morris had been drunk and out of control.

'That doesn't excuse his behaviour, sir. He has done nothing but harrass me since I got here. I could've died because of him.'

'Well, Miss Malik, I intend to look into this matter. Morris might be my son, but, you're right, he can't get away without being reprimanded. Your job is still here if you wish to work with us.'

'Can you guarantee Morris won't bother me again?'

Mr Rhodes nodded gravely and said.'I shall see to it personally that nothing like this ever happens again.'

Not wishing to burn all my bridges, I decided to stay on. Good jobs were difficult to come by and why should I be the one to suffer when Morris had done all the groping?

I thanked Mr Rhodes and told him I was going back to Bradford for my mum's wedding. I'd be back at work in a few days' time.

I left the building feeling relaxed. I wasn't out of a job after all!

Saturday dawned bright but cold. Mum looked gorgeous. I watched her walk down the aisle and for the first time in my life, I was really proud of her. The service was boring. Outside on the church steps the photographer wanted us all to smile as we posed.

Mick came over and hugged me. 'I'm glad you're back on your feet.'

I replied, 'I wouldn't have missed it for the world.'

Arif looked good in a suit. He came and stood by my side. 'Hey Stacey, one day that could be you and me.'

'Yeah, sure,' I said thumping him.

After the reception, Mum and Mick started saying their goodbyes. Sammy stood with her mum, beaming from ear to ear, a hand on her stomach.

'Mum,' I called. 'Don't forget your bouquet.'

'I almost forgot,' she laughed. 'Right, you lot, stand back.'

Turning the other way, she raised the bouquet over her head. I got ready for it. As it soared through the air, somebody shoved me out of the way. Swearing like a trooper, I saw Arif, arms outstretched, catch the bouquet.

'Yeah man!' he said triumphantly.

Everyone roared with laughter as he held onto his trophy. 'You little piglet!' I snapped. 'I really wanted that.'

'Sour grapes, eh?' he eyed me.

As we waved Mum and Mick off on their honeymoon to Paris, he put his arm casually around my shoulders and said, 'Let's make a deal Stacey, you go out with me and I could be persuaded to give you this.'

He shoved the bouquet under my nose.

I whipped it out of his hands, hit him over the head with it and ran off. Our shouts of laughter could be heard all over the hall as he chased after me.

When everything had quietened down, I sat in my bedroom and smiled to myself. Things had worked out okay. Now all I had to do was keep Arif off my back and carry on with the rest of my life. A knock on the door shook me from my reverie.

'Hey Stacey,' Arif popped his head round the door. 'Won't you reconsider please?'

My pillow narrowly missed his head!